DEATH AT THIRTY FATHOMS

The Japanese destroyer hounded the *Swordray* through every evasion. Depth charge after depth charge shook the hull, and the explosions were getting closer. The ship's battery was running low and Commander Holmes knew any moment might be their last . . .

His decision was immediate.
"We don't have a snowball's chance in hell if we just sit here. They've got us dead to the rights. The only chance we have is to fight our way out."

Bantam Books by Clay and Joan Blair

MISSION TOKYO BAY
SWORDRAY'S FIRST THREE PATROLS

THE
SUBMARINERS

SWORDRAY'S
FIRST THREE PATROLS

Clay & Joan Blair

BANTAM BOOKS · TORONTO · NEW YORK · LONDON

THE SUBMARINERS: SWORDRAY'S FIRST THREE PATROLS
A Bantam Book | June 1980

ISBN 0–553–13653–4

Published simultaneously in the United States and Canada

Bantam Books are published by Bantam Books, Inc. Its trademark, consisting of the words "Bantam Books" and the por-
trayal of a bantam, is Registered in U.S. Patent and Trademark
Office and in other countries. Marca Registrada. Bantam
Books, Inc., 666 Fifth Avenue, New York, New York 10019.

PRINTED IN THE UNITED STATES OF AMERICA

0 9 8 7 6 5 4 3 2 1

MOTTO:
Courage Runs Deep

THE
SUBMARINERS

SWORDRAY'S
FIRST THREE PATROLS

Chapter One

1

Commander Hunter B. Holmes, U.S. Navy, captain of the fleet submarine *Swordray*, sat alone in the miniature wardroom, sipping coffee and reading the *Honolulu Post Dispatch*. He was a handsome man, thirty-six years old, blue-eyed, blond-haired, tall and angular. He read the news of the war in Europe and Africa with undivided attention, but the story that held the greatest interest for him was one datelined Washington. It was an account of the arrival in Washington of a Japanese special envoy, Saburo Kurusu. The story speculated that Kurusu might be bringing new proposals for the peace talks going on between Japanese Ambassador Kichisaburo Nomura and U.S. Secretary of State Cordell Hull.

Holmes read this guesswork with skepticism. He had long since concluded these diplomatic talks were futile. The new prime minister, Tojo, was as bellicose as Hitler or Mussolini. Holmes felt he would never about-face and pull out of Indochina. Each day, Tojo's statements mounted in ferocity. It was only a matter of time.

The topside watch, Seaman Edward Strong, parted the drapes to the wardroom and said, "Excuse me, Captain. There's an armed guard messenger from the *Holland*."

The armed guard, wearing a holstered forty-five pistol, presented Holmes with a heavily sealed manila envelope. Holmes signed the chit and, after the two men had

left, pulled the passageway curtains shut, tore open the
envelope, and pulled out the papers. They were stamped
TOP SECRET. In his fifteen years in the navy, Holmes
had never received a message marked TOP SECRET.

He read:

TO: Commanding Officer, *Swordray*
FROM: ComSubRon Two

SUBJECT: Unit Movement

1. In accordance with CNO TOP SECRET Dispatch 41/7125–6, Submarine Squadron Two will
prepare for immediate departure to Manila, P.I.

2. All vessels will maintain a war footing. . . .

The order was two pages long, tightly crammed with
technical instructions for the movement. It was signed
"W.E. Doyle, Commanding." Holmes read it twice, with
mounting incredulity. The entire squadron—twelve fleet
boats and the tender *Holland*—to Manila! What the hell
was going on? The squadron was the backbone of the
Pacific Fleet scouting force. Was the fleet to be utterly
stripped of its submarines? It made no sense.

There was another distressing factor—a personal one.
Fearing the onset of war, Holmes had recently sent his
wife Helen and his two children back to the States. They
had settled in San Diego, reasonably close and reachable
by air even on short leave. Manila was an added five
thousand miles away. The air service from there was
infrequent and uncertain. There was no telling when he
might see his family again.

The passageway curtain parted again and *Swordray*'s
executive officer, Lieutenant George W. Phillips, entered.
Five years younger than Holmes, Phillips was dark-haired
and dark-eyed. He was athletically built, a handsome
bachelor. In Holmes' view, he was the most competent
younger officer in the sub force.

"Good morning, Captain," Phillips said cheerily, sitting down at the baize-covered table. He spoke with a
trace of a Southern drawl. Leroy Collins, the black mess

steward, served him a cup of coffee. Holmes decided to wait a moment before exploding the bomb.

"How was your weekend?" he asked.

Phillips sipped his coffee thoughtfully. "It was everything a sailor could want, Captain. Have you ever been to Kona? It's a beautiful place. Paradisiacal. Black sand beaches. The house party was elegant. The food was marvelous. The ladies were lovely. But somehow, flying back this morning, I felt empty. Maybe I'm getting . . . beginning to feel my age."

Holmes eyed his exec with amusement. As the sub force's most eligible bachelor, Phillips was envied by most of the naval officers in Pearl Harbor. "Come now, George," he said, "you've had too much partying this weekend. What you need is a few days of good hard work, or an interesting new assignment."

"No, Captain. I'm serious. I really envy you Helen and the kids. I'd get married and settle down in a minute, if I could find a girl who wasn't empty-headed and only wanted to party all the time." He sipped his coffee, then added, "*If* this things blows over."

"I wouldn't do anything hasty," Holmes said. "Take a look at this." He shoved the TOP SECRET document across the table. Phillips read with widening eyes. "Manila!" he exclaimed in a tone of disbelief. "*Why?*"

"I don't know," Holmes said.

It was monumentally puzzling. After a ten-year technical and political struggle, the sub force had finally earned an accepted place with the Pacific Fleet. The boats would scout ahead, reporting on enemy forces and movements and, when ordered, torpedo targets of opportunity. That was why they were now designated "fleet submarines." But the fleet was not going to Manila.

Holmes found out the answer to Phillips' question that afternoon when Captain "Red" Doyle summoned the twelve submarine skippers of his squadron to a conference on the *Holland*. Doyle was a man of few words. "General MacArthur and Admiral Hart," he began, "have convinced Washington that with additional forces they can stop an invasion of the Philippines on the beaches. We're being sent out as part of the general land, air and sea buildup."

Holmes spoke right up. "You mean as coastal defense?"

"Yes," Doyle scowled, obviously irritated by the question.

There was good reason for irritation. Forty-one years ago, in 1900, the first short-legged, gasoline-powered submarines had been bought by the U.S. Navy solely as "coast defense" weapons, an extension of coastal artillery. But in World War I, the Germans had proved how effective the submarine could be as an *offensive* weapon on the high seas against merchant ships and warships. Germany's antishipping submarine offensive had very nearly defeated Britain and had earned the submarine a permanent place in all naval forces. It was insulting to the assembled submariners—who dreamed of sinking carriers and battleships—to learn that they were to be relegated to a 1900-type mission: beach defense in the Philippines

"Are there any more questions?" Doyle asked testily.

There were none. Each skipper was too preoccupied mulling over this demeaning new assignment, this sweeping turnabout in naval tactics, and the considerable disruption to their personal lives that the deployment to Manila entailed.

2

Holland led the way into the glinting blue waters of Manila Bay. She was the grand old lady of the sub force. Inside her bulky, grey-camouflaged hull were, in addition to spacious quarters for the SubRon Two staff and ship's company, machine shops, optical shops, torpedo shops, all manner of shops for submarine refit and repair—plus enormous storage spaces for fuel oil, torpedoes, ammunition and food. She was like a miniature, compact, floating navy yard, manned by the finest submarine technicians in the U.S. Navy.

Behind her the two divisions of six submarines, painted black, steamed in surface formation, two abreast.

Salmon. Seal. Skipjack. Snapper. Swordray. And so on. By order of Red Doyle, all hands wore whites in honor of the arrival. It was not a popular order. Aboard ship, submariners customarily wore dungarees. The order had led one *Swordray* seaman to crack, "New battleship reporting to the Asiatic Station. *U.S.S. Swordray.*"

Hunter Holmes, resplendent in starched whites, took the conn on the bridge. The Officer of the Deck was Lieutenant (j.g.) Henry Slack, the boat's first lieutenant. He was Naval Academy Class of 1932, a football hero in his senior year (all-American halfback) and still built like one. Tom Bellinger, the quartermaster, was a greying, oldtimer who also served as chief of the small quartermaster-signalman gang. Bellinger was the only one of the three who had been west of Pearl Harbor.

Holmes swept the panorama unfolding before them with binoculars. To port, distantly, he could see the fortress Corregidor and the rugged green hills of the Bataan Peninsula. To starboard, distantly, he could make out the radio towers of the Cavite naval base, and to the north of that, a pall of smog hanging over Manila. He viewed it all with a mounting sense of excitement and wonderment. He thrived on new places, new experiences. Now it was to be the mysterious Far East. Manila, "The Pearl of the Orient."

He turned suddenly to the quartermaster, Bellinger. "You've been out here before, haven't you?"

"That's right, Captain," Bellinger said. "My first enlistment. Nineteen hundred and twenty-four. Came out with the *Canopus* in the deck gang. Put in six years on her, making eighteen bucks a month."

Canopus was another submarine tender. She had been in the Asiatic Fleet ever since the mid-1920s, mothering six World War I vintage "S" class boats. She was still in Manila, Holmes knew. She was now tender not only for the S-boats, but also eleven older fleet boats that had been sent to Manila much earlier, in 1939 and 1940.

"How'd you like it here?" Holmes asked.

"In those days," Bellinger said, "it was the best goddamned duty in the fleet." It seemed very distant to him now, a time with no relation to the present. He had

been very young, very reckless. He felt lucky to have
survived the fleshpots of Manila. And Shanghai. And
Hong Kong.

"Ship dead ahead, sir." The report came from Ed
Strong, one of the two lookouts in the periscope shears. He
added, "Several ships. Destroyers. Heavy cruiser."

They all examined the oncoming formation with binoculars. "It's the *Houston*," Bellinger said. "And light
cruiser *Marblehead*." He counted the destroyers. "Thirteen
tin cans."

"The *entire* Asiatic Fleet surface force," Henry Slack
amplified, with no small contempt. "What the hell do they
think they can do with that puny outfit? They wouldn't last
thirty minutes."

Holmes fixed his binoculars on the *Houston*. He had
to agree with Slack. The 10,000-ton *Houston*, with a
battery of nine eight-inch guns, was already eleven years
old and badly in need of modernization. The light cruiser
Marblehead, with a battery of twelve six-inch guns, was
eighteen years old. The destroyers were World War I
vintage four-stackers. The Asiatic Fleet might be useful
for showing the flag, but it would be useless against the
Japanese Imperial Fleet.

After the naval formation passed abeam and formal
salutes had been exchanged, *Holland* reduced speed and
maneuvered toward the Manila waterfront. As they approached the city, they found the bay crowded with
merchant ships and sampans of all nationalities. Dutch.
Thai. Burmese. Chinese. Australian.

"There's *Canopus!*" Bellinger reported with a note of
excitement. She was moored at the waterfront, wearing a
new coat of battle grey. Three old black-hulled S-boats were
nested along her port side.

According to the plan, *Holland* moored at a waterfront pier. For security reasons, her twelve subs anchored
well offshore and doubled the topside watch. Red Doyle
was obsessed with the fear that saboteurs might damage
the boats. As a further security precaution he decreed
there would be no trading with the native boats hawking
fresh fruit and vegetables and native crafts.

Soon after *Swordray* dropped the hook, yet another
message came from Red Doyle. All submarine command-

ers would report immediately to *Holland* for a conference with Admiral Thomas C Hart, Commander, Asiatic Fleet.

3

Admiral Hart met each skipper at the wardroom door, shook hands and as he repeated the skipper's last name aloud, committed it to memory. He was short, jut-jawed, feisty and sharp as a tack at age sixty-four. He was extremely handsome, the very picture of what an admiral should look like. When Hunter Holmes put out his hand, the admiral's blue eyes flashed and he said, "Holmes? Class of twenty-six?"

"Yes, sir," Holmes replied, astonished that the admiral would know his class year.

"Aren't you married to Roy Lowman's daughter?" Hart said. "Mary Ann?"

"The older one, sir," Holmes said, still astonished. "Helen."

"Of course," Hart said. He frowned and went on. "I was sorry to hear about Roy. He was a fine man. CNO material."

"Thank you, sir," Holmes said. "With your permission sir, I'll tell Helen you said that."

"Very well, Holmes," Hart said. "Welcome aboard." He then turned to the next skipper in line, extending his hand.

Holmes took a seat at the huge, baize-covered wardroom table. He watched as Hart's aide set up some maps of the Far East on easels and a lectern. When the last skipper had paid his respects, the admiral moved from the door to the lectern. His aide handed him a pointer. Hart was all business.

"War," he began crisply, "could come at any hour—any moment. This command is on full war footing. I want each and every one of you to conduct yourself according-ly."

They had read that in the newspapers. The Asiatic Fleet had been more or less on a war footing since mid-summer when the Japanese gobbled up Indochina.

Hart had pulled most of his ships—and the U.S. Marines —out of China. He had sent all the dependents back to the States, a tough order that led to howls of protest on the floor of the House of Representatives and elsewhere. It instantly made him the most unpopular admiral in the Navy.

"General MacArthur commands the land and air forces," Hart went on. "He's an eternal optimist. He doesn't agree with me. He thinks the Japs have spent themselves in China and don't have the capability of launching a war against the Philippines until at least April 1942. He's trying to build the Filipino Army to two hundred thousand men by that date. If the Japs are kind and thoughtful enough to hold off an attack until then, he intends to stop them on the beaches. This is an important change in our strategy and one reason you are here. Now, I assume you are all familiar with the old War Plan Orange?"

They all nodded silently and respectfully. Every senior naval officer was not only familiar with War Plan Orange but steeped in its various aspects. War Plan Orange was an outgrowth of the theories of the naval strategist Admiral Alfred Mahan, who held that wars between great naval powers would be decided by one massive sea battle. War Plan Orange was the naval plan for the defeat of Japan. It assumed that a Japanese attack against the United States would commence in the most vulnerable area: the Philippines. In such an event, according to Orange, the small U.S. Army garrison in the Philippines and the Asiatic Fleet would blunt the initial attack, then fall back to the Bataan Peninsula and Corregidor, the island citadel at the mouth of Manila Bay. Its huge guns would prevent the Japanese from occupying Manila Bay and utilizing it as a base. Meanwhile, the U.S. Pacific Fleet would proceed west to defeat the Japanese Fleet in a single decisive battle.

"Plan Orange," Hart went on, "is out the window now. At least the Army side of it. No retreat to Bataan and Corregidor. It's now a self-sufficient, stand-and-fight strategy. A key element, of course, will be air power. Washington has promised General MacArthur one hundred Flying Fortresses and three hundred new fighters.

With a force of that size he is confident that he can maintain air superiority and defeat any attempted Japanese landing." He spent the next fifteen minutes at the maps, showing with the pointer how MacArthur's fledgling Filipino Army (which would include regular U.S. Army units and legions of "advisers") would be deployed for combat. Then he returned to the lectern.

"Now," he resumed, "let us turn to the role of the Asiatic Fleet. As you know, it is not much of a surface force. *Houston, Marblehead* and thirteen destroyers old enough to vote." He paused for the laughter. "But," he went on, "we, too, are being reinforced. The British have sent the battleship *Prince of Wales* and the battle cruiser *Repulse* to Singapore. The Australians and Dutch are contributing heavy and light cruisers and destroyers. In event of hostilities with Japan, all American, British, Dutch and Australian surface naval forces will be merged into a single hit-and-run fighting fleet designed to delay the Japs until the Pacific Fleet arrives." For the next ten minutes, he ran through the order of battle of these combined forces, listing ships by type and name.

At the conclusion of his briefing on the surface forces, Hart asked for questions. There were several, mostly regarding availability of supplies, fuel oil and ammunition. These were stored at the Cavite naval base, the admiral said. It struck Holmes as curious that reserve stocks had not also been stored elsewhere, just in case. But his question was in another area.

"Admiral," Holmes said when Hart had acknowledged his raised hand, "have the various naval units of the four nations conducted joint maneuvers?"

"No," Hart replied. "It is a delicate political situation. We are not legally at war. Washington believes it would be a provocative act against the Japanese to conduct joint maneuvers. But I understand your import and it is well taken. Off the record, we are making plans for secret maneuvers. But that's not to leave this room."

On the whole, Holmes concluded to himself, the surface naval end of the defense of the Philippines as described by Hart was disquieting. Too few ships. No dispersal of stores. No joint maneuvers. It impressed him as more hope than substance.

Hart continued. "I know what each and every one of you is thinking. The naval plan is inadequate. I lie awake every night with that same thought. Let us now turn to your role—the role of the Asiatic Sub Force—in the defense of the Philippines."

He paused for dramatic effect. "Gentlemen, frankly, submarines are the key. The role of the Asiatic surface force will be merely diversionary, designed to split the enemy's forces or tie up a certain number of ships. Our twenty-nine submarines will be the *main* offensive arm of the Asiatic Fleet. It will be up to you to cripple or stop the Japanese Imperial Fleet. *You* will sink his capital ships and his troopships. Play absolute havoc until the Pacific Fleet can get here. To my knowledge, no submarine force of this size and caliber has ever been assembled in one place." He went on, describing what they knew very well—the order of battle of the Asiatic Sub Force— stressing repeatedly that it was the chief offensive arm of the Asiatic Fleet. When he was finished he invited questions. There were many.

"Sir, what is the exact plan for deploying the submarines?" Freddy Warder, skipper of *Seawolf*, asked.

"That has not been decided," Hart said. "Now that you are here, a war plan incorporating all six S-class and twenty-three fleet class boats will be formulated."

Holmes asked, "Sir, where will we get information on Japanese fleet and troopship movements?"

"From all the usual naval intelligence sources," Hart replied. "But our best source will be General MacArthur's Flying Fortresses. Some will be outfitted for reconnaissance missions."

"Has that been coordinated with the Army Air Corps, sir?" Holmes went on. Neither he nor any other of the skippers had ever needed to depend on a separate service for intelligence information. This, too, was disquieting.

"No," Hart said. "But it will be. Soon. The Flying Fortresses have only just arrived—as you have only just arrived."

Johnny Burnside of *Saury* spoke up, as usual, a bit too forcefully. "Admiral, as I see it, we are being asked to play a role here that we're not trained to do. A coastal defense role, really. Coordinating with another service to stop an invasion force close to the beaches. Speaking for myself, sir, I've got grave doubts about the effectiveness of that role. We're trained to operate with the fleet on the high seas. . . ." There were nods and murmurs of agreement among the skippers.

Hart fixed them all with a stony glare. "A Naval Academy graduate is trained to be flexible in his thinking, Burnside. Resourceful and opportunistic. To go in harm's way. Upon you depends the fate of seventeen million Filipinos, intensely loyal to America. Remember, gentlemen, the American flag flies here. It will continue to fly here until the Filipinos are granted independence. I will hear no further discussion about your role. I expect each of you to do his duty to the utmost."

He stopped, staring directly at Burnside, to let that sink in. Then, in a wholly different mood, he concluded the conference. He smiled tightly and said, "You and your wardrooms are cordially invited to a reception at the Manila Hotel at five o'clock tomorrow night."

Chapter Two

1

The five officers on *Swordray*—Holmes, George Phillips, Henry Slack, the engineering officer, Fred Bohlen and the communications officer, Bill Nolan—shared a cab from the waterfront fleet landing to the Manila Hotel. Although it was late November, the beginning of the "cool" dry season, they found the teeming city sweltering. As bad as the Canal Zone. They mopped their brows with handkerchiefs and hoped they would not get sweat stains on the armpits of their tunics.

The Manila Hotel was one of the city's most luxurious buildings. The grand old hotel had been modernized with a new five-story wing. As they debarked from the taxi, Holmes said, "I heard MacArthur and his new wife live on the top floor of the new wing. An air-conditioned suite, furnished with priceless antiques."

"I heard he keeps a sixteen-year-old Filipino mistress," Henry Slack said as they mounted the veranda steps. Slack had an uncanny ability to arrive in a place cold and within one day know where all the bodies were buried. He was a born gossip, an endless—and often valuable—source of amusement and information.

The reception was already underway in the grand ballroom. Admiral Hart and his staff, dressed in immaculate whites, were deployed in a long formal receiving line. The Asiatic Fleet orchestra played softly from the stage. The room itself was decorated with tropical flowers, primarily orchids and ferns. The officers of *Swordray* joined the long line. They shuffled slowly toward the heavy brass, thankful for the air-cooling system and the sluggish ceiling fans.

There was a girl immediately ahead of George Phillips in the line. She was wearing a silk print dress and white gloves and carried a white evening purse. Her perfume, Chanel Number Five, was his favorite. From the back, her figure seemed lovely. Small, taut buttocks, fine legs sheathed in silk stockings. She had lush brown hair shaped into a pageboy. She seemed to be alone.

She turned suddenly, as though she felt his eyes on her back. Phillips was momentarily stunned. She was beautiful. Liquid brown eyes. Pale skin. Pert nose. Full-breasted. She extended a gloved hand and said in what Phillips took to be an English accent, "Hello. I'm Anne Simpson. You must be from the new squadron, one of the guests of honor?"

Phillips shook her hand, astounded at his good fortune. "That's right. George Phillips, *Swordray*. May I present my captain and the other officers?" He introduced Holmes and the others. She shook hands with each, gracefully and charmingly.

She said to Phillips, "We're very glad to have you in Manila. It's one more indication that the president's commitment to defend the islands is a real one."

The line was inching along. She turned and shuffled forward a pace or two. Following her, Phillips thought desperately how to continue the conversation. "Are you English?" he asked.

She turned again, smiled and said, "No. I'm American. But I've only lived in the States four years. I grew up in London; went to school abroad."

"What are you doing way out here?"

"I'm in the Political Affairs section of High Commissioner Sayre's office," she said.

Phillips nodded. He was going to ask, "Secretary?" But he swallowed that question. She was obviously nobody's secretary.

He looked again at her gloved hand, to see if there was a wedding ring. He could not tell. "How'd you happen to be in London—and spend all that time in Europe?"

"My father's with the Foreign Service," she said. "He's now the ambassador to Costa Rica."

"Oh, I see," he said. "Ambassador Simpson?"

"Yes," she said, smiling at his subtlety. She went on, "I'm in the Foreign Service, too. I'm here because I speak the language and Commissioner Sayre is an old friend of my father's." She turned around again. They were approaching Admiral Hart, the head of the receiving line.

Catching sight of her, the admiral beamed and said with uncharacteristic feeling, "Anne! You look lovely tonight."

She shook his hand, bent to kiss Hart's cheek and said, "Thank you for inviting me."

"I'm honored you accepted," the admiral said, blue eyes twinkling. He passed her on to the next officer in line, his chief of staff, with, "I'm sure you know Admiral Rockwell. . . ."

She did, noted Phillips, who was listening intently. Phillips gave his name to Admiral Hart's aide, then shook hands with the admiral, next with Admiral Rockwell, then the whole long line of Asiatic Fleet captains. He observed that Anne Simpson appeared to know them all quite well. And they her.

When they reached the end of the line and were cast adrift in the milling crowd, Phillips said, "May I get you a cocktail?"

"Yes, thank you," she said. "A daiquiri, please."

She watched him make his way to a waiter carrying a silver tray of cocktails and highballs. He was handsome, she thought. Thirtyish. Bright. Southern. Very attractive. But probably married, with several little ones back in the States. She had met too many lonely sailors far from home ever to get involved with one. To her, they were all alike. All out for a good time. All trying to live up to the "girl-in-every-port" reputation of the U.S. Navy.

He returned with two chilled daiquiris and gave one to her. He raised his glass and said, "As we say in London, cheers!"

"Cheers," she returned, sipping her drink. "What part of the South are you from?"

"Mobile, Alabama," he said.

"Damn the torpedoes, full speed ahead," she laughed.

He laughed in return.

"Is there a Navy tradition in your family?" she asked.

"No. Just me and my great grandfather. He was an admiral in the Confederate Navy. All the rest of the Phillips men were—or are—lawyers." He paused, then added, "Tell me about Manila. What do you do for fun out here?"

"I'm afraid I'm the wrong one to ask," she said. "Other than official duty parties, like this, I don't go out much."

"What do you do in your spare time?" he asked.

"I don't *have* much spare time," she said. "Our office is short-handed. We're all swamped with work."

"All work and no play . . ."

She cast him a quick stern look that compelled him to break off the trite adage. He shifted ground quickly and said, "Tell me about your work. Exactly what do you do?"

That question seemed to mollify her. She started to tell him in some detail. Phillips hung on every word.

2

Quartermaster Tom Bellinger went ashore with the senior enlisted man on *Swordray*: Jack Lyons, the chief of the boat. They had to wait until the liberty launch called at *Swordray* on one of its endless circling rounds. It was a long ride to the beach. The boat stopped at *Sturgeon*, *Sargo* and *Sculpin* before going on to the fleet landing. All hands involved in this lengthy pickup process were unanimous in the opinion that Red Doyle's security precautions were a lot of shit.

As they climbed ashore, grumbling, Bellinger looked at his watch and said to Jack Lyons, "One hour and twenty minutes! To hell with this battleship-navy routine. We'll have to find our own boat and set up a private liberty run and pickup service."

"Exactly what I was thinking," Lyons said, waving to the next cab in line. He was a lean, dour man, a motor machinist with sixteen years in submarines, and family problems he refused to discuss with anyone other than Bellinger. They were plankowners. They had helped commission *Swordray* in late 1938 and served on her ever since.

"God, it's hot in this town!" Lyons said when they settled in the sagging back seat of the taxi.

"Rosaria's," Bellinger said to the driver, "Calle d'Oro."

Bellinger was a tough-minded sailor, but now, back in Manila after these many years, he was almost overwhelmed by nostalgia. Flashback after flashback assaulted his mind. He sat in uncharacteristic silence, watching familiar sights go by, remembering. It had changed very little. It was still hot. Still dirty. Still mysterious. Still wild.

"You're sure this place—Rosaria's—is okay?" Lyons asked.

"It's clean," Bellinger said.

"I hear the SPs are off-limiting a lot of these joints," Lyons said.

"So I hear," Bellinger said. "But not Rosaria's. She runs a classy joint."

The cab turned down Calle d'Oro—Street of Gold— threading through heavy, noisy traffic. This was the brothel-bistro district. The sidewalks teemed with merchant ship and man-of-war sailors, soldiers and airmen. Filipino barkers energetically worked the doors of the strip joints. Here, years ago, Bellinger grew to manhood.

The cab stopped at number sixty-nine Calle d'Oro. It still looked the same to Bellinger. Nothing more than a heavy, ornately carved, teak door. There was no barker, no outward sign of what went on behind the door. He paid the exorbitant fare in American currency and they got out and rang the bell. A small panel in the upper part of the door opened to reveal the face of a Filipino man.

"Name?" he said.

"Bellinger," he said, adding quickly, "I go way back."

The panel closed. They waited a full three minutes, Jack Lyons grumbling skeptically and impatiently. Then the panel opened again and a plump woman's face appeared. She studied Bellinger a moment, then shouted, "Tom!"

The door swung open. "Rosaria!" Bellinger exploded lustily embracing the fat, heavily-scented woman. His mind swirled with memories.

"This is Jack Lyons," he said, breaking away.

"Con mucho gusto," Rosaria smiled, showing gold fillings and extending her hand. Lyons shook hands and nodded silently. She turned back to Bellinger. "Where have you been all these years? You look marvelous! Not a day older. Look at me. I've grown old and fat." She paused and added, "But rich." She cackled.

She led them down a long, dank, stone corridor into a large rear, open-air, garden patio. It was lush with tropical greenery and little trickling colored waterfalls. Here and there were rattan, candle-lit tables. Young, olive-skinned, Eurasian girls in silk dresses sipped champagne at the tables and talked sexily to Navy chiefs and a scattering of Army and Air Corps sergeants. Somewhere off-stage, a jukebox played soft Glenn Miller.

Tom Bellinger took it all in at a glance. "Nothing has changed," he said to Rosaria.

"Except for the prices," Rosaria corrected, grinning. "I see you are first class and are qualified in submarines. You have *mucho dinero,* no?"

"Sí," Tom said. *"Mucho dinero."*

"Come," she said, taking his hand. "We must first catch up."

She led them to an empty table. A Filipino waiter in white jacket appeared immediately. Rosaria said to Bellinger, "This one's on me. Still V.O. and ginger?"

"No," he said. "Bourbon on the rocks."

"Tell me all," Rosaria said when the waiter had taken the order.

Bellinger, in his humorous and self-deprecating way, briefly sketched what had happened to him over the last ten years. Rosaria nodded enthusiastically and smiled and barely touched her champagne. Jack Lyons, monumentally bored looked dourly around the patio, sizing up the girls. When Bellinger finished, she said, "Still not married?"

"Nope," Bellinger said.

"Poor Tom," Rosaria said to Lyons, feigning pity. "He almost . . ."

She stopped abruptly, breaking off the recollection. Bellinger smiled tightly, remembering. Her name was Juannita.

"Why aren't you two at the Admiral's reception?" Rosaria bantered, moving quickly off the subject.

"You know I despise those formations," Bellinger bantered back. "Stuffy."

"A fine man, that admiral," Rosaria said. "He did me the greatest favor in the world."

"What's that?" Bellinger asked.

"He sent all the wives home," she said, again cackling. "Business increased twenty-fold."

Bellinger and Lyons laughed. "Where are you putting all your money?" Bellinger asked.

Rosaria leaned forward and lowered her voice. "Not in Philippine banks, for sure. I convert it to gold and jewels. I'm what you Navy men call highly mobile."

"You're ready to run?"

"You're damned right," she said emphatically. "That MacArthur's a dreamer. The Filipino Army! Meet them at the beaches! Bah! What a joke. Kids. Green kids. They don't know how to fight and they don't have anything to fight *with*."

"But we've come to save you, Rosaria," Bellinger said.

"Too little, too late," Rosaria quoted sadly. "War will come soon. Maybe next week. In his mind, your president has written us off. It will be a disaster."

"Where will you run to?" Bellinger asked.

"Singapore," she said. "The British will fight to the last man. But, enough of this. You didn't come here to talk to me about the damned war. I have the perfect girl for you, Tom."

3

"Would you like to dance?" George Phillips said to Anne Simpson. He had not left her side since they met in the receiving line.

The reception had loosened considerably with the

flow of liquor. The orchestra had shifted from muted classics to lively swing; the level of conversation from subdued to noisy.

"No, thank you. I really must be going," she said. "I have a very busy day tomorrow."

"May I see you home?" he asked, clearly disappointed.

"Thank you," she said, "but I have a driver waiting." She extended her hand. "It was nice meeting you."

"Wait ... Please ... I'd like to see you again. Can you spare a few hours tomorrow to show a stranger around Manila?"

"I'm sorry. . . ."

The orchestra suddenly trailed off to dead silence and Admiral Hart stood before it at a microphone. "Ladies and gentlemen," he said in a deep, formal tone. "May I please have your attention? Thank you. I'm pleased to inform you that I've just received word that General Douglas MacArthur and his wife Jean will be joining us. The general would like to say a few words of welcome to the men of SubRon Two."

The admiral applauded and all those in the room followed his example. At the height of the applause, MacArthur and Jean entered the ballroom, as if on cue. All eyes turned to observe this famous soldier striding ramrod-straight toward the stage, with Jean double-timing along behind. Hunter Holmes was astounded. He had seen MacArthur once, in Washington, in 1931, when he wore four stars and was Chief of Staff of the United States Army. He had not aged a bit. He was now sixty-one (as Holmes knew) but he looked twenty years younger. He wore no hat. His hair was a deep even brown, as though dyed. He wore enough ribbons to decorate a platoon of soldiers.

When he had mounted the stage alongside Hart, the admiral said, "Ladies and gentlmen, I give you Lieutenant General Douglas MacArthur, Commander Army Far East Ground and Air Forces."

MacArthur, holding himself as if he had a flagpole for a spine, moved to the microphone and spoke. "Men of SubRon Two, welcome to the Philippines. I'm sure by now Admiral Hart has briefed you on our new strategy. The

Army and Navy Departments are sending a steady stream of Flying Fortresses, fighters, artillery, tanks, ammunition. I am rapidly expanding my network of airfields and beach defense works. By April first, I shall have fielded a well-trained Filipino army of two hundred thousand men, with more than adequate equipment. If the Japanese should attempt to invade the Philippine Islands, I shall meet them on the beaches, and I shall prevail. The enemy will be stopped in his tracks. Destroyed!"

He paused dramatically. The ballroom again erupted in applause. When it died down, MacArthur resumed. "I welcome from the bottom of my heart the arrival of your twelve new submarines and the tender *Holland*. This new increment almost doubles the existing Asiatic submarine force. I fought in Europe in World War I and I am well aware of the enormous lethality of the submarine. Your fleet boats are the most sophisticated and powerful weapons in the history of naval warfare. Should the need arise, I know you will give a good account of yourselves. God protect you and give you a fair breeze."

Then he was gone.

George Phillips, slack-jawed and a bit overwhelmed, stood beside Anne Simpson. "My God," he breathed.

"Isn't he magnificent?" Anne rhapsodized. Even though she had seen MacArthur many times in private and public, he invariably stunned her with his eloquence, bearing, confidence and erudition.

"He comes on a bit strong," Phillips said. "Like an actor—a regular John Barrymore."

"That's true," she conceded. "It's part of his technique. But deep down, he's genuine. A military genius. He's done more for the Filipinos than anyone in the world. And they love him."

Phillips smiled at her earnestness. "Now, as I was saying. Can you spare a few hours to show a stranger around Manila? How about lunch tomorrow?"

"Look, Mister Phillips," she said pleasantly. "This has been lovely. But don't waste your time on me. You'll meet lots of young women who'd be thrilled to show you the sights. I really am terribly busy at the office right now." She paused, looked at him frankly and finished, "There's

no room in my life right now for play. Good night and
good luck."

She turned and strode off, gracefully, purposefully,
nodding to various admiring Asiatic Fleet brass as she
made her way to the door. Phillips stood rooted, watching
her get away. Defeated, yet refusing to concede defeat.

Hunter Holmes walked up to his exec and said
lightheartedly. "So you struck out, for once?"

"I have not yet begun to fight," Phillips quoted,
grinning broadly. "Let's get a drink."

4

The girl Rosaria picked for Tom Bellinger was named
Maria. Jack Lyons chose another named Angela. They
were both young, light-skinned, refined Eurasians, the pick
of Rosaria's litter. The four shared a bottle of expensive
champagne at the patio table, then split up and went to
separate rooms upstairs.

The rooms were better appointed than Bellinger remembered. Much better. Red satin bed sheets! He set the
bottle of bourbon on the nightstand by the bed and
watched Maria slip daintily out of her dress. She had the
body of a sixteen-year-old. Smooth and taut, firm, small
breasts.

He poured a drink and said, "Where are you from,
Maria?"

"Shanghai," she said. "Hong Kong." She remained
standing and naked.

"Shanghai," he said. "The greatest city in the world."

"No more," she said. "Terrible now."

He took off his black neckerchief and pulled off his
jumper and sat on the bed. She sat beside him, very
upright, and caressed his neck. "You and Rosaria old
friends?" she said.

"We go way back." He took the pack of cigarettes
from his socks and put them on the table and began
unbuttoning the thirteen buttons on his trousers.

"She's fine madam," she said. "Strict but fair."

"How come you left Shanghai?" he asked.

"I was sent away when the war came," she said. "To a convent in Hong Kong."

He smiled to himself. He had heard the convent story a hundred times. He pulled off his shoes, socks, skivvy shirt and trousers and lay back on the bed in his shorts.

"You're a submariner?" she said.

He nodded, lighting a Lucky Strike.

"From the new boats?"

He nodded again.

"Which one?"

"*Swordray.*"

"I know many submariners," she said proudly. "From *Perch, Porpoise, Pike, Permit.*" She named all eleven of the older fleet boats in the Asiatic Fleet. "Submariners good men. Very brave. They all come here on paydays."

He inhaled deeply, remembering the paydays in the old days. Rosaria. Juanita. Especially Juanita.

"*Swordray* is newer?" she asked.

"Much newer," he said. "The newest."

"How many torpedo tubes?" she said, nestling against him. "Six? Eight?"

He was going to say, "Ten—six forward and four aft," but he checked himself. He could not remember if the information had been publicly released. Instead he said, "Enough to do the job."

She pulled off his skivvy shorts and began caressing his body with her tongue. She was very skillful. He crushed out the cigaret and pulled her against him hard. She was the best he had known for a long time. Afterward, he sipped his bourbon and smoked another Lucky Strike. She cuddled close, fondling him tenderly.

"You are built very big," she whispered. "Like a Mark Fourteen!"

He chuckled. "You know a lot about submarines!" Perhaps too much, he thought.

"You have the Mark Fourteen torpedo on your boat?" she cooed in his ear.

"You ask a lot of questions," he said. "You shouldn't. Dope like that is classified."

"I love submariners."

"Maybe . . ." he said, changing the subject. "What will you do if the war comes here?"

"Join the sub force," she laughed. "With me aboard *Swordray,* you couldn't lose."

"You can say that again." He tried to picture that.

Then, suddenly serious, she said, "President Quezon will make a deal with the Japanese. The Philippines will be neutral. You have no worry. You'll see."

They had sex again. Afterward, while he drank and smoked, she asked, "Why do you anchor out in the bay?"

"Security," he said. Then, "No more questions."

Later, he dressed and went downstairs and had a drink with Rosaria, waiting for Jack Lyons. He said to Rosaria, "Maria was very good."

"But not as good as Juanita?"

"No. Juanita was one of a kind."

"Did you really love Juanita?"

"What is love, Rosaria?"

"You ask *me!*" she cackled loudly, shrugging her shoulders.

"What happened to Juanita?"

"I thought you'd never ask," Rosaria said. "She married an Australian copra planter from New Ireland. Rabaul. She's a lady of means now—and quality."

"Then she's better off," he said. "And that's a good thing for her." He paused, tossed off his drink and said, "Where'd you get Maria?"

"She just walked in—about a year ago. From Hong Kong."

"The convent story," he said, nodding.

"Her parents were killed by the Japs in Shanghai," Rosaria said somberly.

"I'll bet," Bellinger said sarcastically, lowering his voice. "I don't believe a word of it, Rosaria. She asks a hell of a lot of technical questions about submarines. Way, way out of line."

Rosaria seemed disturbed by the implication.

"I'd watch her closely," Bellinger went on. "Don't trust her. If the Japs come, you might find your throat cut and Maria in charge."

"You think she could be a *spy?*" Rosaria whispered, eyes big as saucers.

"Manila must be crawling with Jap spies," he said. "With this military build-up going on? Hell, they'll want to know everything."

She sipped her champagne, frowning. "Everything is changing so. Day by day. I feel like I live on quicksand. Tom, what do *you* hear? Are the Japs coming?"

"You hear more than I hear, Rosaria," he said. "You tell me."

"There's a lot of talk around that Quezon's made a non-aggression pact with the Japs," she said.

"That's ridiculous," Bellinger said. "He can't do that without an okay from Washington. They'd never okay that."

"That's what I thought."

"Well, don't believe it."

She was still very concerned about Maria. "I could get rid of her just like that," she said, snapping her fingers.

"You want me to have O.N.I.—Naval Intelligence—check her out for you?"

"Can you do that?"

"No sweat," he said. "I'll put in a chit."

"You're still the same old wonderful Tom," she smiled, putting her hand fondly over his. "How I love you! I'm so glad you're back."

"No, I'm not the same, Rosaria," he said. "I'm getting old and tired. And a little scared."

Jack Lyons came down the stairway arm in arm with Angela. He was actually beaming contentedly. They settled the huge accounts in American currency, called a taxi and returned to the fleet landing.

Chapter Three

1

The *Holland* gig, gleaming with a new coat of white paint, pulled alongside *Swordray* at 0730. Hunter Holmes leaped adroitly aboard and took a seat in the amidships salon. There were already seven SubRon Two skippers in the gig: Charlie Freeman of *Skipjack*, Ray Lamb of *Stingray*, "Bull" Wright of *Sturgeon*, others. Holmes sat beside Ted Aylward of *Searaven*, a classmate and an old friend.

"What's this all about?" he asked Aylward. Red Doyle had called yet another conference of his skippers.

"Not a clue," Aylward said sleepily.

The gig went from sub to sub until it had collected all twelve skippers. Freddie Warder of *Seawolf* had heard a startling and scandalous rumor that possibly explained this latest in a seemingly endless series of conferences. "I heard Red Doyle got falling down drunk at Admiral Hart's the other night. *That* didn't sit too well with the admiral. The word is Red could be on the skids—on his way out."

"I heard that, too," Holmes said quietly. The word had come to him from Henry Slack, who had heard it from a classmate on the SubRon Two staff.

They debarked onto *Holland*, filed up to the ward-room and took seats at the big table. They had met so often lately that each now had his own special place. Presently, a clutch of brass entered the room: Red Doyle and two other four-stripers. One was John Wilkes, who had been, until the arrival of SubRon Two, Commander, Sub Force Asiatic Fleet. Rumor had long held that Doyle was to relieve Wilkes, who had been in Manila three years and was due for shore duty in the States. The skippers rose, or started to rise, but Doyle said, "At ease. As you were. Keep your seats."

The three captains—each with a briefcase—took seats reserved for them at the center of the table. Doyle opened his briefcase, removed a sheaf of papers stamped "TOP SECRET," laid them on the table before him and said, "This meeting carries a classification of TOP SECRET. *Nothing* is to leave the room."

He picked up the top paper, put on his glasses and said, "In the last three days, Admiral Hart has received two dispatches from Admiral Stark in Washington, both of utmost gravity. The first on November 24, the second today." He read the first one:

CHANCES OF FAVORABLE OUTCOME OF NEGOTIATIONS WITH JAPAN VERY DOUBTFUL. THIS SITUATION, COUPLED WITH STATEMENTS OF JAPANESE GOVERNMENT AND MOVEMENTS THEIR NAVAL AND MILITARY FORCES INDICATE IN OUR OPINION THAT A SURPRISE AGGRESSIVE MOVEMENT IN ANY DIRECTION INCLUDING ATTACK ON THE PHILIPPINES OR GUAM IS A POSSIBILITY.

He laid the message aside. The skippers looked at one another in wide-eyed amazement. Doyle picked up another dispatch and said, "This came in today." He read:

THIS DISPATCH IS TO BE CONSIDERED A WAR WARNING. NEGOTIATIONS WITH JAPAN HAVE CEASED . . . . AND AN AGGRESSIVE MOVE BY JAPAN IS EXPECTED WITHIN THE NEXT FEW DAYS . . . AGAINST EITHER THE PHILIPPINES, THAI OR KRA PENINSULA OR POSSIBLY BORNEO. EXECUTE APPROPRIATE DEFENSIVE DEPLOYMENT.

The skippers sat in dead silence, staring at Red Doyle. Holmes had a terrible feeling of unreality. He had known it was coming, but now that it was here—or almost here—he could not properly register it on his consciousness. It was like a movie, a fantasy.

"All right," Doyle went on, laying his glasses on the table, wearily wiping his eyes. "As some of you may have guessed, I was to relieve John Wilkes. Admiral Hart has decided that since John has been out here three years and knows the territory, it would be inappropriate to make a change at a crucial time like this. John will remain Commander Asiatic Submarines, with the temporary rank of commodore; Squadron Two will be formally incorporated into his command."

So, Holmes thought, the rumor was true. Red Doyle was on the way out, professionally ruined; never to be selected to admiral; soon to be banished to the limbo of passed-over captains. That Hart was one very tough cookie.

"I will now turn these proceedings over to Commodore Wilkes," Doyle said, returning the TOP SECRET papers to his briefcase.

John Wilkes, a handsome officer with a commanding presence, spoke right up. "As temporary commodore, I now rate a chief of staff. He is James Fife, who arrived by air from Pearl Harbor last night. He has most recently been in London, where he was able to talk his way aboard a British submarine, and make a war patrol in the Mediterranean."

All eyes fell on the third four-striper in the center of the table, James Fife. He was a wizened, stern-looking officer in rumpled khakis that seemed much too large for him. Holmes had never seen him before, but he knew he was a legend in the submarine force. Once a hard-drinking sub skipper, Fife had given up all alcohol, divorced his wife and "married the Navy." In the late thirties, he had commanded the sub school in New London and washed out one-third of the class. He was a sundowner, a humorless martinet with large ambition and—reputedly—a sharp intellect. Upon his introduction, Fife merely nodded briskly, showing absolutely no emotion, not a trace of warmth or comradery.

Wilkes went on, "I know you will be happy to know that Admiral Hart and I have formulated the submarine operational plan. Basically, it is as follows. Upon the declaration of war, one-third of the boats will be sent on the high seas to attack the Japanese naval forces at their major staging bases: Formosa, Indochina, the Palaus. One-third will be deployed around the perimeter of Luzon to scout and intercept invasion forces that may slip by the boats on the high seas. The other one-third will be held in strategic reserve in Manila Bay to be launched against the main invasion force, when it is found."

For the next two hours, Wilkes described the many details of the plan. It sounded reasonable, and even logical, but it was a radical shift from what they had been trained to do. They would not be with the fleet, but widely dispersed across thousands of miles of ocean, all alone, or else scattered around Luzon, close to the beaches. Holmes did not like it. It seemed a violation of the basic tenet of naval warfare: never divide your forces, concentrate power in one major effort. But neither he nor any of the other skippers challenged the plan. Clearly it had been dictated by Hart, down to the smallest detail. You didn't buck four stars in this man's Navy. You played it strictly by the book.

"Finally, gentlemen, there is one more item, not small," Wilkes went on in his grave, formal way. "Torpedo exploders. I'll put this in writing later today, but I wanted you to know it's coming. You will shift from the Mark Five exploder to the Mark Six. These will be issued to you tomorrow. It has been downgraded by the Bureau of Ordnance—BuOrd—dispatch from TOP SECRET to SECRET. Familiarize yourself, your torpedo officer and torpedomen in the use of the Mark Six as quickly as possible."

A hush fell over the room. It was as though Wilkes had mentioned the unmentionable. In fact, he had. The Mark Six magnetic torpedo exploder was the most closely held of all the Navy's weapons secrets. So closely held that heretofore to mention it, even in disguised language, was a general court-martial offense.

The open discussion of the Mark Six that ensued intensified Hunter Holmes' feeling of unreality. Years ago, after his first tour of sea duty as a boot ensign—three years on the *Pennsylvania*—he had applied for a post-graduate course at the Naval Academy. The tour had been granted in part because his father-in-law, then Rear Admiral Roy Lowman, was superintendent of the Academy and wanted Helen (and the baby) to live on the grounds. Holmes had chosen ordnance engineering for advanced study and as a work-study project, had been assigned to a minor role in placing the Mark Six magnetic exploder into limited—and highly secret—production at the Navy's Torpedo Station in Newport, Rhode Island. It had been so hush-hush then—and afterward—that he had not been able to explain to Helen what he had been doing in Newport.

Holmes had learned a great deal about the exploder, all there was to know, in fact. He knew far more than any other skipper in the *Holland* wardroom. It was a device initially conceived to offset the trend of surface men-of-war to acquire more and more side armor, making them impervious to torpedoes. The magnetic exploder was designed to set off the torpedo *beneath* the ship, triggered by the electrical forces inherent in the magnetic field of the target vessel. Since most men-of-war were only lightly armored at the keel, or not armored at all, it was believed that a torpedo exploded beneath a warship would break its back.

Wilkes had just got to that point in his briefing. "Gentlemen, the Mark Six magnetic exploder is the most revolutionary weapon the Navy has ever produced. You will be able to sink a heavily-armored battleship with one or two torpedoes. They'll never know what hit them. Even if they do find out, it's too late. There's no way they can armor-plate their keels at this late date. Thus, as a naval weapons system, the fleet submarine with Mark Six exploders has achieved parity with the battleship—or even exceeded it."

Almost mesmerized, they pondered this wondrous statement. One submarine might go on patrol and sink two, three, four battleships and cruisers. It was fantastic!

Hunter Holmes then remembered something he had not thought of for ten years. A gnawing doubt returned after all this time. The Mark Six had been exhaustively tested in the Newport laboratory and declared absolutely reliable. But there had been only one, highly-controlled, "live" test, and that was not against a battleship. In the late 1920s, the Navy had been strapped for funds and was afraid of a security leak. After repeated requests from the exploder designers for a "live" test, the Navy begrudgingly authorized one and made available a small, old submarine, *L-8,* which was bound for the scrap heap. The sub was moored in Newport harbor and two torpedoes were fired at it from a shore-mounted torpedo tube. The first failed to explode, but the second blew *L-8* to oblivion. No further tests were ever made.

Four years after that, when Holmes was involved in a small way in putting the Mark Six into limited production, he had heard the *L-8* story. It seemed unbelievable to him that such an important device had not been more thoroughly tested—at least fired from a real submarine at sea against a substantial target. He had even drafted an official letter to the project officer urging more extensive live tests. But the project officer would not endorse the letter and turned it back with the comment: "We don't rock boats in BuOrd." Since the project was so highly classified, Holmes was unable to express his concerns through other channels. He could not even discuss it with his father-in-law. Ultimately, he put his worries out of his mind and merely hoped for the best.

He now spoke up. "Commodore, do you know if the Mark Six has been live-tested recently?"

Wilkes stared at him as though he were a lunatic. Then he said coldly. "BuOrd would not issue a weapon to the fleet that had not been live-tested. As a Gun Clubber, you ought to know that."

Holmes responded. "Sir, I played a small role in the production phase of the Mark Six." He went on to explain his role and what he had heard about the testing—the *L-8* story. The wardroom listened, transfixed. Holmes concluded, "In my opinion, sir, it might be a good idea to conduct our own live tests right here in Manila."

Wilkes stared incredulously, then exploded. "Using *what* for a target, Holmes. *Holland?*"

"Perhaps the admiral could provide us a target," Holmes said, not backing down. "An old vessel due for scrapping."

"Holmes, you're completely out of order," Wilkes said angrily. "Completely. I'll not have you undermining confidence in this weapon with ten-year-old information—

all hearsay. Gentlemen, I repeat, BuOrd would not supply us a weapon without its fullest endorsement and that *has* to mean it's been tested—and tested and tested. The sub force is going to hold the Philippines with the Mark Six."

Again a hush fell over the room. This time it was an embarrassed hush. Holmes was crimson around the collar of his tunic, boiling with anger. But he said nothing further.

"What about a manual, sir?" Freddie Warder said. "When do we get the manuals?"

"There are no manuals," Wilkes said.

Holmes remembered that story, too, from years back. The Newport torpedo station had prepared one manual. But it was considered so sensitive that it was locked away in a safe. It had never been published for fleet distribution, even after the exploder was made operational.

"Sir," Holmes said quietly, "I think I could prepare a manual. Something, at least, that could serve as a temporary manual."

"Very well," Wilkes said stonily. "You do that Holmes. One copy for each of the twenty-three fleet boats, one for *Holland*'s torpedo shop. Twenty-four copies and that's all. Classify them SECRET."

"Aye, aye, sir."

There ensued an interminable discussion about tactical use of the Mark Fourteen torpedo fitted with the Mark Six exploder. Wilkes was explicit on the main point: Torpedoes would be set not for contact with the sides of the targets, as they had practiced all their careers with the Mark Five contact exploder, but to run deep beneath the keel. Thirty or forty feet, depending on type of vessel. The rest would be magic. Wondrous magic.

2

At 1100, George Phillips gave up waiting for Holmes to return from *Holland* and prepared to go ashore. He had a single aim—to find the High Commissioner's office and Anne Simpson and take her to lunch, or if not that, dinner. In the ten days since they had met at the reception,

Swordray had been at the Cavite navy base undergoing engine repairs. Phillips had not been able to get the girl out of his mind. It was like a mysterious oriental fever. He had never been so thoroughly smitten.

He called for the skiff and went topside. The skiff—along with its fifteen horsepower Evinrude outboard motor —had been mysteriously acquired by the chief of the boat, Jack Lyons. It was exclusively *Swordray* property, used for running people back and forth to *Holland* and the fleet landing. Phillips knew better than to ask how Lyons had acquired it. Navy chiefs were famous for getting things done out of channels. You did not ask them how.

The quartermaster, Tom Bellinger, had liberty and was also headed for the beach. Phillips and Bellinger shared the ride. Seaman Strong operated the boat, in return for being relieved of all watch-standing duties.

"You must be fairly well connected in these parts," Phillips said cheerily to Bellinger as they rode along.

"Know my way around Calle d'Oro," Bellinger said with a grin.

"So I heard," Phillips said, returning the grin.

"Expensive as hell now," Bellinger said, shaking his head. "Everything's ten times what it was in the old days." He thought fleetingly of Juanita, then he looked at Phillips, silently appraising.

Bellinger had not much cottoned to Phillips when he reported on board *Swordray* a year ago in San Diego. He came across as a little too much the social playboy for Bellinger's taste. Their assigned duties had thrown them in close company. As exec, Phillips was also ship's navigator. As leading quartermaster, Bellinger was assistant navigator. Phillips' navigation had been rusty; he had not really trusted Bellinger's. It had been an awkward accommodation for both. Gradually, Bellinger had changed his mind about Phillips. He saw a lot of intelligence and a good quick mind. In time, Bellinger concluded, Phillips would rise to his own command and, with seasoning, make a very good skipper. One of the best.

"Old Man at another *Holland* conference?" Bellinger asked.

Phillips nodded. "His daily penance, it would seem."

"Captain Doyle sure likes to confer, don't he?" Bellinger said. He added quietly, "I heard he put on quite a show up at the admiral's quarters the other night."

My God! Phillips thought, mildly shocked. How far had that story spread? All over the sub force? He did not reply. The subject was barely whispered in the wardroom. By no means would it do to discuss—or even acknowledge it—to an enlisted man. Even one as discreet as Bellinger. He changed the subject. "Did you get those charts and the Title B stuff? The binoculars?"

"Got the charts," Bellinger said. "Such as they are. But I'm having a problem with the binoculars. Shortage on *Holland*. Somebody fucked up in Pearl. Forgot to load a batch. But they've been found in the warehouse and are supposedly en route on the *Pensacola*. She's escorting a convoy out here. Meanwhile, I've got six pair on loan."

"Loan!" Phillips laughed. "You can't *lend* Title B equipment."

Bellinger winked. "An old buddy of mine runs the binocular shop."

Phillips said no more. It was unorthodox, but at least the Old Man would no longer be harassing him about the damned binoculars.

Seaman Strong brought the skiff alongside the fleet landing with great skill, squeezing in ahead of a bulky liberty launch from the cruiser *Houston*. Phillips and Bellinger jumped out and waved for two taxis, just ahead of the mob of *Houston* sailors. When Phillips asked the driver if he knew how to get to the High Commissioner's office, he nodded vigorously and said, "All drivers know how. Very big shot place."

The driver tore through unknown, teeming, city streets at breakneck pace, veering, slamming on his brakes, blowing the horn and cursing in Tagalog. Phillips hung on tightly, fearing for his life. Finally they screeched to a stop before a Spanish-style mansion set in a park-like oasis. Phillips was doubtful until he saw a small discreet temporary sign: "U.S. High Commissioner," and a U.S. Marine sentry on the veranda by the huge teak doors. He paid the fare and walked up the stone walk. The sun was high; it was humid, sweltering.

The Marine, who wore a holstered forty-five, snapped to attention and saluted. When Phillips returned the salute, the Marine politely asked his business.

"I'm looking for Miss Anne Simpson," Phillips said. "Political Affairs Section."

"Yes, sir," the Marine returned smartly. "Second floor. Turn left. Fourth door on the right."

"Thank you, Corporal," Phillips said as the Marine pulled at the massive door to admit him.

The door opened into an enormous tiled foyer in the center of which rose a wide flight of stone stairs. Everywhere American civilians rushed to and fro on urgent business. From every office he could hear the clacking of typewriters or people shouting into telephones. He mounted the stairway, wondering whose mansion this had been. It seemed very old and had no doubt seen much colonial history.

At the top of the stairs, he turned left down the corridor and almost collided headlong with Anne Simpson. She was rushing along with an armload of folders.

"Well *hello!*" she said, mind racing feverishly to place him. Hart's reception. Alabama. Damn the torpedoes. George. George Phillips. *Swordray*.

"Hi," Phillips said, cheerily doffing his cap. "I just happened to be driving by and thought I'd say hello." She was wearing glasses, but behind them, she was as fabulous as he remembered. He noted in a quick glance that she was not wearing a wedding or engagement ring.

Anne shifted the folders into her arms like schoolbooks. She was caught by surprise and a bit flustered, curiously unsettled by the sight of him. "You see? I wasn't kidding," she said. "We really *are* busy."

"Can I help you carry those files?" he asked.

"No. Let me put them away. Then I'll show you around."

She rushed into an office, leaving him standing alone in the busy traffic. A minute later she was back, unconsciously pushing at her hair, thinking she must look a mess.

"Can you get away for lunch?" he asked.

She laughed. He did not give up easily. "We don't really go to lunch, or take a siesta. We eat together in the rear patio. Sort of a working lunch." She was aware that she was explaining unnecessarily. She looked at his ring finger. He wore an Annapolis ring, but no wedding band. Not many sailors did wear them, she reminded herself.

"You couldn't possibly get away?" he implored. "Just this once?"

She hesitated, looking at him frankly, then at her slim, gold wrist watch. "I really shouldn't," she said, "but, okay. Just one hour. All right?"

"Great," Phillips said.

They took a cab to a small Italian restaurant that she knew and liked. The maitre d' recognized Anne and gave them a prime table in the shaded patio. They ordered frozen daiquiris and antipasto and veal sautéed in a light wine sauce.

"Cheers," Phillips said, raising his glass.

"Cheers," she returned. Then her face clouded. "Have you heard the news from Washington?"

"What news?" he said.

"The war warning," she said in a low voice. "The negotiations have been broken off."

"War warning?" he said skeptically.

"Yes. Admiral Hart received it last night."

He frowned. "I hadn't heard." That would explain the long conference on *Holland*. Yet *another* alert. He had better return directly to *Swordray* after lunch. "If war comes, what will you do, Anne?"

"Do?" she said. "Keep on with my work. Peace or war, one does what one is assigned to do."

"But . . . I meant, if there is an invasion?"

"They will hold the beaches," she said confidently. "You heard General MacArthur. There's no way the Japanese can take the Philippines."

He thought momentarily about that. His views had been influenced by Holmes' cool and analytical evaluation of the war plan. There was great doubt in his mind that MacArthur's green, ill-equipped, conscript Filipino Army could hold at the beaches. But he kept these doubts to himself and said, "There might be bombing."

"We have shelters," she said. "We've had drills."

Phillips abruptly shifted the subject away from war.

"Is it true that President Quezon is a very sick man?" he asked.

"Yes," she said sadly. "He has T.B."

"What happens politically if . . . ?"

She frowned. "That's what I'm trying to sort out this week. Believe me, it's very complicated."

They gradually slid away from serious talk to light banter. She inquired about his career and he about her schooling in Europe. Time flew. Before they had half-finished the meal, she looked at her watch and exclaimed in alarm, "I've been gone an hour and a half!"

He grinned. "I know." He put his hand on hers and added, "You worry too much and work too hard. You needed a break."

The touch of his hand stirred something deep inside her. She looked down at his hand, then at him, and said in her frank way, "George, are you married?"

"No," he said. "Dedicated bachelor. And you?"

"No."

"No time?" he teased. "Too busy?"

"No one ever asked me," she said, again nervously looking at her watch.

"That's hard to believe," he said, signaling for the check.

"I could say the same about you," she said. "How come some Southern belle didn't snare you?"

"None ever asked me," he said, grinning, as he paid the check. Then he added seriously, "Nobody in her right mind should marry a sailor. Not a submarine sailor anyway. Not if they're smart and think about it. A lot of them rush in willy-nilly—and then they're sorry."

They made their way to the street and flagged a taxi. When they were settled inside, he took her hand in his lightly. Again she felt a deep stirring, a queer, disquieting sensation.

He said gently and very earnestly, "May I see you again?"

She looked at him for a moment. He didn't *seem* to be just another lonely sailor on the make. He seemed to be serious. And besides, by this time she was strongly attracted to him. "Yes," she said. "That would be nice."

Involuntarily, she gently squeezed his hand. He returned the squeeze, feeling a vast sense of ease, contentment and happiness. Anne Simpson was an extraordinary woman, he thought.

3

Tom Bellinger taxied to the Marsman Building in downtown Manila. Admiral Hart had established Asiatic Fleet headquarters ashore here so as not to encumber his war-ready flagship *Houston*. The Asiatic Fleet staff shared the building with a branch of the Sixteenth Naval District, which had its main headquarters at Cavite. Bellinger showed his I.D. to a Marine sentry and went inside to study the directory. He found that the O.N.I. division of the Sixteenth Naval District was located on the third floor. He took the elevator to the third floor and soon found the office. It too was guarded by Marine sentries who, at first, refused to admit him.

"I want to see Chief Farland," Bellinger said.

That seemed to be a magic password. The Marine stepped aside, opened the door and told Bellinger where to find Chief Farland. Bellinger signed the visitors' logbook and entered the office.

Farland, a rotund man with silver hair and pink cheeks, presided over a large bull pen of enlisted men who were busy with file folders and typewriters. As Bellinger walked through his open door, Farland was talking on the telephone and gazing out large windows overlooking the city. When he turned and saw Bellinger, his blue eyes widened in amazement and he slammed down the telephone and jumped up, extending a hand.

"Tom Bellinger!" he shouted. They shook hands warmly.

"I heard you were still here," Bellinger said. "Christ, you must be completely Asiatic."

They had served together an infinity ago on *Canopus*. After the first hitch, Bellinger had gone back to the States and to the boats. Farland, a yeoman striker, had remained in Manila, going to the Sixteenth Naval District headquarters. They had grown up together on *Canopus*—and Calle d'Oro. They chatted a moment about old times and what had happened in the last ten years. Farland, it seemed, had had a good Navy life. He had married a Filipino and had four children. He had been chief for three years, a minor record of achievement. Then they got down to business.

"You remember Rosaria?" Bellinger said.

"Rosaria? Rosaria who?"

"On Calle d'Oro," Bellinger said. "You remember. A very classy joint."

Farland furrowed his brow, then smiled. "Haven't set foot on Calle d'Oro in six, seven years, Tom."

"Rosaria runs the best place on the street," Bellinger elaborated. "Expensive, but good. Always had the best girls. Lot of submariners hang out there. In the old days—and now."

"Yes," Farland replied. "I remember faintly." But clearly, he did not. Nor did he understand what Bellinger was getting at.

"This town must be full of spies," Bellinger said.

"That it is," Farland said, nodding confidently, sweeping a pudgy hand toward the bull pen. "We've got a file on all of them."

"There's a gal down at Rosaria's," Bellinger said, "asking a hell of a lot of technical questions about submarines when she gets you in the sack. I think she ought to be checked out."

"Oh yeah?" Farland said, now quite interested. "What's her name?"

Bellinger gave Farland what information he had. Something Chung, went by the name of Maria. (All of Rosaria's girls were given Spanish Christian names.) Shanghai. Convent. Parents killed. Hong Kong. Manila. Walked in off the street. Farland jotted notes on a pad.

"Pretty slim," Farland said, frowning, making a final note.

"And probably none of it true," Bellinger said.

"Exactly," Farland said. "But I'll check her out. I've got a civilian team working Calle d'Oro. Pretty good boys."

"How long will it take?" Bellinger said.

Farland squinted. "What's your interest in this, Tom? Other than security?"

"Rosaria's an old friend," Bellinger said.

"Oh," Farland said. "Well, okay. We'll see what we can do. Give me a week, ten days."

"Appreciate it," Bellinger said.

"Appreciate your tip," Farland said. He paused again, lowered his voice and said, "Did you get the word? Last night Washington sent the admiral a war warning. That's off the record, by the way."

"War warning!" Bellinger echoed, thunderstruck.

"Negotiations are broken off," Farland confided. "This may be it."

"They might hit us here?" Bellinger asked. "The Philippines?"

"Any day," Farland said.

"What about this MacArthur?" Bellinger asked. "Can he stop them?"

Farland sneered. "He's a pompous ass. Publicity hound. The Filipino Army couldn't fight its way out of the proverbial paper bag. Until the fleet gets here, it's really going to be up to you guys—the submarines."

"Well," Bellinger said, forcing cheer, "don't worry. They tell me the Jap Navy ain't worth shit."

"I wouldn't be too sure of that," Farland said. "The dope O.N.I.'s putting out makes 'em look pretty good."

Bellinger felt a strong sinking sensation in the pit of his stomach. A fear. He rose, shook hands and somberly left the office. On the street, he flagged a cab and went to Rosaria's, where he was recognized by the hall porter and admitted instantly. Rosaria was sitting at a table in the patio drinking tea. When she saw Tom, she jumped up excitedly and exclaimed, "Tom! Welcome! How was Cavite?"

He sat down, ordered a drink. "Cavite hasn't changed."

"Awful place," Rosaria shuddered.

"Busy place," Bellinger said. "They haven't got the manpower. We had to do most of the work ourselves. Nobody ever got off the base."

"Poor Tom," Rosaria cooed, smiling sweetly, placing her hand on his.

Bellinger sipped his drink slowly, looking over the girls at the tables. He was the only customer present. "Client," as Rosaria now rather grandly called them.

She lowered her voice. "Have you heard about the war warning?"

He said, "Now who the hell told you about *that?*"

"It's all over town," she said, shrugging. "Everybody knows. All the cab drivers—*everybody*."

"Some security," Bellinger said disgustedly. "We leak like a sieve."

"We've had these alerts before," she said. "The summer of forty. Last summer. But this time, I'm really worried."

"This could be the real thing," he conceded somberly. "Where's Maria?"

"I don't know," Rosaria said, glumly, frowning. "She worked night before last, but she was not here yesterday. *Or* today."

"She's left for good?"

"Your guess is a good as mine," Rosaria said. "They're not supposed to leave without my permission. So . . ." She shrugged again.

"I put a chit in on her," Bellinger said. "We're checking her out."

"Thanks so much, Tom," she said, squeezing his hand. "But I'm afraid it may be too late."

"They'll find her," he said. "They know Calle d'Oro pretty well. We'll see."

They sat in silence for a moment. Then she said morosely, "This is it, isn't it, Tom? They're coming?"

"I honestly don't know," he said. "It *could* be, Rosaria. It could be."

"There's a Dutch ship leaving for Singapore in the morning," she said. "Something tells me I should take it. What do you think?"

He stared a moment into her dark eyes. They were clouded with fear. He said, "Rosaria, I couldn't advise you, one way or another. It might blow over. Then again, it might not. It's a decision you have to make yourself."

"I could always come back," she went on, clearly agonizing. "For months, I've had this guy on my back. He wants to buy me out. Ten thousand gold dollars in cash. I could sell and leave. If it blows over, I could come back and open up an even better place."

Bellinger felt pity for her, but he was determinedly neutral. "That's one possibility," he said.

"You're no help!" she sighed in exasperation. Then with sudden resolution, "I'm going to do it! Every bone in my body says *go*."

"Then go," he said.

"I'm going," she repeated. "Tomorrow morning."

They sat in silence for another moment. Then she said, "I want to ask a big favor of you, Tom."

"Yes. Sure. What is it?"

She lowered her voice to a whisper. "Come back here tonight. I'm going to entrust something to you for safe-keeping."

"All right," he said.

"I've got to tend to business now," she said, suddenly rising. "You want a girl?"

"No. No. Not now."

"Maybe tonight?"

He grinned and said, "Trying to milk a last few dollars out of your old running mate?"

She cackled. "It'd be on the house." Then she rushed up the stairs to her private quarters.

Tom spent the rest of the day sightseeing, drinking and leisurely attending to small chores. The most important of the latter was a fitting for two sets of tailor-made whites. He ordered the top of the line and paid the big bill in advance. He had a late lunch alone in a fine Chinese restaurant, during which he wrote six post cards, including one to his mother, then returned to pick up his uniforms. By six o'clock, he was back at Rosaria's. The hall porter led him up to her private quarters.

"Good," she said urgently. "I knew I could depend on you, Tom."

Her bedroom was crowded with closed steamer trunks and suitcases. She poured him a drink. He sat down on a chaise and said. "So you sold out and you're really leaving?"

"Yes," she said. "I made that bastard give me *twelve* thousand gold dollars!" She cackled. He sipped his drink, amused at her business shrewdness.

She sat down on another chaise, suddenly highly agitated, wringing her hands. "Twenty years! Now it's *his*. It's a terrible wrench, Tom. Terrible."

"Of course," he said, trying to soothe her. "Anybody would feel the same way."

She perked up a bit at that and said, "Now, the favor."

She got up and walked to a steamer trunk. On top of it was an ornately-carved teak chest with equally ornate brass hinges and locks. She patted the top of the chest. "It's all in here, Tom," she said. "My life's work. Fifty thousand in gold and jewels." She paused, frowned, then went on. "I can't take it with me. I'd surely be robbed. Probably killed. I want you to take it, Tom. Take it on *Swordray*. Hold it for me. Okay?"

Bellinger stared at Rosaria in utter amazement. When he found his voice, he stammered, "But . . . I can't . . . I mean . . . There's no place to put it. . . . What if there's a war? Where would I ever find you? What . . . what if we're sunk?"

She dismissed his questions with a smile and quick flip of the hand. "Will you do it?" she pressed.

Bellinger took a deep breath. "Yes . . . but . . ."

"Don't worry," she said with a mischievous grin. "I'll always know where *you* are. You'll hear from me when I'm settled."

Bellinger collected himself and repeated, "But what if we're sunk?" He thought, but did not say, what if something happens to you?

She shrugged. "Bring the box. I'll get a taxi."

The box was very heavy. Bellinger muscled it down to the street where Rosaria was waiting with a cab and the porter with Bellinger's package of new uniforms. He put the box on the back seat and took the package from the porter. Rosaria hugged him tightly and kissed him on the cheek. *"Hasta luego,"* she said.

He climbed into the cab and pulled the door shut. She was weeping. "What's the name of that Dutch ship you're taking?" he called to her out the window.

"S.S. Piet Heyn," she managed.

"Hasta luego," he called out as the taxi pulled away. She waved.

Chapter Four

1

Exactly at the moment George Phillips reached the fleet landing, the heavens opened. He raced to the dock in a driving downpour, silently cursing. Seaman Strong was waiting in *Swordray*'s private skiff, wearing foul weather gear, the Evinrude idling. After Phillips had climbed into the boat, Strong let go the line, put the motor in gear and sped out into the choppy waters of the bay.

For the past ten days—ever since the November 27 war warning—liberty on *Swordray*, as on the other boats, had been severely curtailed. The officers and enlisted men had been divided into two watch sections, port and starboard. One third of each watch section was granted liberty from 1300 to 2100—eight hours—every other day. By the captain's orders, these men were now forced to take the regular liberty launch. Use of the skiff had been restricted to the five chief petty officers and the five officers. Thus Seaman Strong's ferry work had been cut to the point of being a boondoggle.

His most frequent and regular passenger these days was the exec, who was still free to come and go as he pleased. Like the captain, Phillips stood no watches. Every day for the past ten days, he had left the ship at precisely 1300 hours in the skiff and every night at precisely 2400 hours he had arrived at the fleet landing for the return trip.

The reason for Phillips' arduous liberty schedule was soon apparent to the crew. More than a half-dozen of them had seen him in this restaurant or that, in company with a stunning female. Through comparing notes, it was established that it was always the same girl. Mister Phillips seemed to be on cloud nine. In all this scuttlebutt, the real news was not that he was seen with a good-looking girl, but that it was always the same girl. Was the dedicated bachelor finally hooked?

Seaman Strong became a primary source of the scuttlebutt. During the nightly return trips the two men chatted idly. Never about the girl, but Strong was a shrewd judge of mood. Without ever asking a question, he could tell how the evening had gone. Most had gone exceedingly well, although on two nights Phillips was cranky.

A quarter mile off the beach, the rain abruptly stopped, the water smoothed, and the skiff settled down.

"Nice night," Strong volunteered.

"Lovely," Phillips said. Strong surmised that the exec, in spite of being soaked to the skin, was deliriously happy. "Lovely," Phillips repeated, staring at the sky which was now clear and packed with stars. Definitely another good night, Strong thought.

Strong picked out the dark silhouette of *Swordray* and made a minor course adjustment. Seeing that low-slung black silhouette, Phillips felt an inner surge of pride. She was the most complicated weapons system in the history of warfare; sleek and deadly. He had tried to express his feelings about *Swordray* to Anne, but he had become tongue-tied. It was not something he could put in words. It was a *feeling* a man had for a ship, a very special feeling a man had about a submarine. Women could not understand it and it was a waste of time to try to explain it.

They pulled alongside the bulbous saddle tanks. Phillips jumped on the tanks and nimbly scrambled up onto the wood-slat deck, saluting the double topside watch. Then he turned back to Strong who was lashing the skiff's painter to a limberhole in the side superstructure. "Thanks, Strong," he said.

"Aye, aye, sir," Strong said, as he had for ten nights running. "Glad to do it."

Phillips went forward to the hatch leading down to

the forward torpedo room. Ducking below, he smelled the peculiar and warm belowdecks aroma of a submarine: diesel oil mixed with cooking smells. His ears picked up the familiar sounds of various humming machinery. By these noises, he could tell all was well.

The torpedo room was dimly lit. There were six bronze torpedo-tube inner doors forward. Inside the tubes were six Mark Fourteen torpedoes, now fitted with the secret Mark Six magnetic exploder. In the stowage racks were ten spare torpedoes—also with the new exploders— gleaming silvery in the half-light. Above the racks there were bunks slung, port and starboard. A dozen enlisted men snored in deep sleep. They were sleeping amidst ten thousand pounds of high grade TNT.

Phillips moved aft, ducked through a watertight door into the forward battery. Beneath the deck lay half of *Swordray*'s powerful electrical storage batteries that provided her submerged propulsion. Above the deck, the long compartment looked like a fancy Pullman car, with roomettes port and starboard. This was officer country—and chief petty officer country. Midway down the darkened passageway, he pulled the drapes aside and entered the wardroom. It was brightly lighted. Hunter Holmes was sitting in his customary chair at the head of the green baize table writing his daily letter to Helen and the kids.

"Good evening, Captain," Phillips said cheerily, doffing his wet cap.

"Hello, George," Holmes said, laying aside his Parker fountain pen, an aging graduation gift, still going strong.

Phillips drew a cup of coffee from the Silex and sat down at the table. He was soaked through. "Raining on the beach," he explained, unbuttoning his tunic at the neck. Holmes waited for more. Tonight, he sensed, there would be much more than usual to report on his affair with Anne Simpson.

Phillips took a sip of his coffee and said with rare gravity and bluntness, "Captain, I need your help. I'm head over heels in love with Anne and I want to marry her, now. But, as you know, Admiral Hart has put out a regulation prohibiting marriages. Do you suppose you could talk him into making an exception?"

Holmes was absolutely floored. He knew Phillips was getting serious about the girl, but he had no idea it had gone this far. Before he could check himself, he blurted, "My God, George, you hardly know her."

Phillips had expected this reaction and had mentally prepared for it. He said earnestly, "I know it looks precipitous, Captain. It is, in a way. And yet it isn't. There has never been a deeper, more profound understanding between two people so quickly. Our minds have merged. It's as though we had been unconsciously waiting to meet, and in this strange set of circumstances, we did. Sir, it's no lark, I assure you. We are *deeply* in love."

Holmes felt monumentally uncomfortable. Never had he been put in such a position. He started to speak, but Phillips rushed on. "Hell, Captain, I'm not a kid. I'm thirty-one years old. I've known hundreds of girls. Nothing like this has ever happened to me. I *know* it's for real."

Finally Holmes spoke, more pompously than he intended. "It's a serious step, George, especially at a time like this. How does *she* feel about it?"

Phillips had dreaded Holmes would ask that. He said quietly, "Truthfully, sir, she says she doesn't want to get married."

"What?" Holmes cried. "Then what's this all about? What . . . ?"

"If I had the permission first," Phillips broke in, "I know I could talk her into it. You see . . ."

"Hold on, George," Holmes interrupted. "The last thing on earth you want to do is *talk* her into it. Especially at a time like this."

There was an urgent knocking on the bulkhead in the passageway, then, "Captain!"

"Yes?" Holmes said. "Come in."

It was the duty radioman, Art Evans, holding an official message form. Since the war warning, Commodore John Wilkes had ordered that all boats in his Asiatic sub force maintain a twenty-four-hour radio watch, even though they were moored in the bay.

"This just came in, in the clear, sir," Evans said, handing over the message. He was pale and shaken.

Holmes read the typed messages:

AIR RAID ON PEARL HARBOR. THIS IS NOT DRILL.

Holmes felt the blood drain from his face. He said, "Are you sure?"

"Yes, sir," Evans said. "It was definitely Pearl. I recognized the keying."

Phillips was greatly irritated by this untimely interruption. "What is it?" he said, a bit testily.

"Oh!" Holmes said. "Here." He passed the message, adding, "Sorry."

Phillips read in disbelief. "Pearl Harbor!" he exclaimed. "What the hell . . . ?"

Holmes turned to Evans. "Contact the *Holland* immediately. See if they picked it up. If not, relay the message exactly as you received it. We want to be sure about this."

"Pearl Harbor!" Phillips repeated in disbelief. "It can't be true! There's been no declaration of war. Anyway, it would be suicidal to attack the fleet that far from Japan."

"Let's go to battle stations," Holmes said, suddenly rising, reaching for his cap. "And you'd better change into dry clothes."

Holmes rushed aft and ducked through a watertight door to the control room, *Swordray*'s nerve center. The belowdecks watch was aft, leaning into the tiny radio shack. Holmes turned the red handle of the battle stations alarm. A soft bonging echoed throughout the boat. The gnawing feeling of unreality returned, but, when the alarm ceased, he picked up the p.a. mike and said coolly, "Men, this is the captain. We've received an unverified radio report of an air raid on Pearl Harbor. We're checking it out. Meanwhile, man your battle stations, take in the mooring lines and put four main engines on the line."

Swordray suddenly came alive. Men fell out of their bunks, barefoot and in skivvy shorts, and ran sleepily to battle stations. Amid the rush, Holmes climbed the ladder to the conning tower, above the control room, then mounted another ladder to the bridge. He saw in the distance that *Holland* was also fully alert, signaling with yardarm blinker lights, repeating the message over and over. So, Holmes thought, it must be true!

The first lieutenant, Henry Slack, who was battle stations officer of the deck, came up on the bridge. He was followed immediately by the quartermaster, Tom Bellinger. Just as they arrived, the four diesel engines burst alive, spewing black smoke from the exhausts aft.

"I have the deck, sir," Slack said, saluting.

"Very well," Holmes said. "Let's get off this mooring buoy."

The deck gang was already forward, unshackling the mooring line from the buoy. Slack cupped his hands to his mouth and shouted, "Deck gang! Step lively. On the double now."

The bridge speaker shattered the stillness of the night. "All hands at battle stations, Captain. Four main engines on the line." It was Phillips, whose battle station was in the conning tower.

"Mooring lines secure," the leader of the deck gang shouted.

"Very well," Slack said. "Deck gang lay below." Then he said into the speaker. "Rig ship for dive."

Holmes admired Slack's performance. A good officer. Cool under stress. In a moment, Slack turned and said to Holmes, "Ready to get underway in all respects, sir."

"Very well," Holmes said. "Back off the buoy and get some sea room."

"The skiff, sir," Slack said. "What shall we do with it?"

"Haul it aboard," Holmes said. "Lash it down."

After this was done, Slack spoke into the intercom. "All back full." Almost instantly there was a great churning of black water off the stern as the two great bronze screws began to turn.

"Left full rudder," Slack said. "All stop. Right full rudder. All ahead one-third." The speaker echoed his commands. Then, "All compartments report ship rigged for dive, sir."

Swordray coasted back, stopped, then gradually moved forward and to the right of the mooring buoy. Holmes turned to Bellinger and said, "Man the searchlight. Tell *Holland* we're underway."

"Aye, aye, sir," Bellinger replied. He climbed into the shears where the searchlight was mounted on a big swivel.

He turned on the light, aimed it at *Holland*'s bridge and rapidly signaled the message.

"Message sent and receipted for, sir," Bellinger shouted down to the captain. He had manned the signal light a thousand, two thousand times in his life, but never with such a sense of urgency. It was all unreal.

Presently, there came another message from *Holland*'s yardarm lights. Bellinger read it aloud. "All vessels this command get underway and await orders."

"We beat them to the punch," Slack said proudly.

Holmes, too, felt a surge of pride. *Holland* had been asleep at the switch. His own report probably prodded them awake and suggested a course of action. If the air raid on Pearl was real, they could expect one here in a few hours—just after dawn. It would not be prudent to be caught at anchor.

2

Never in his naval career had Hunter Holmes experienced such absolute confusion. Orders flowed from *Holland*'s yardarm blinker and were then immediately countermanded by wholly new and different orders. *Swordray's* radio watch intercepted an endless flow of contradictory information. The fleet at Pearl Harbor had completely repulsed a sneak Jap air attack, or the fleet had been destroyed. American Army troops on Oahu had thrown back a Jap landing on the beaches, or the Japs had landed and were marching on Honolulu and Pearl Harbor. In the Philippines, Japanese planes had been spotted off the west coast of Luzon by patrolling Army fighters in a dozen places. But one by one these "contacts" had proven to be false and the fighter scrambles and pursuits a waste of time. Holmes could not believe anything.

Dawn came and went. The expected Japanese air attack on the Asiatic Fleet in Manila Bay did not materialize. Why? No one knew. It was baffling. Perhaps the rumor that President Quezon had made a secret deal with the Japanese was true and the Philippines would remain "neutral." Finally, at 0800, *Holland*, which had left the

Manila waterfront at battle stations and moved out into the bay, seemed to settle down and take charge. She signaled that she was sending a gig to pick up all skippers for yet another conference. Executive officers would take temporary command of the boats. They were to submerge deep enough to get out of sight but keep the "whip" radio antennas above water to receive further orders.

Holmes found the *Holland* wardroom jammed. Not only were the twelve skippers of SubRon Two present, but also the skippers of the eleven older fleet boats and the six old S-class boats. Twenty-nine skippers in total, all talking at once, none with any sound idea of what was going on. Finally, Commodore Wilkes and his chief of staff, James Fife, both grim-faced and red-eyed, entered the room. Wilkes sternly called for silence.

Addressing the assemblage, Wilkes was somber. "Gentlemen," he said, "war has come. At oh-seven hundred Honolulu time, Jap carrier-based aircraft launched a sneak attack on the fleet in Pearl Harbor. The exact extent of the damage is not known. But—and this is highly classified—it would appear the damage may be extensive."

He paused with a pained expression. The skippers sat in absolute dead silence. It was unbelievable that the Japs would attempt a stunt like that against the fleet. Even more unbelievable that they had apparently succeeded. Wilkes went on. "An invasion of Oahu is expected at any hour. Army and Marine troops have been deployed on the beaches. There has still been no declaration of war by the Japanese. That's all I know, for certain."

Again he paused to let the unbelievable news sink in. Then he resumed. "Locally, there have been several verified, unknown aircraft contacts off the west coast of Luzon. However, as you can see, there has been no air attack here. Why, we do not know. In the meantime, General MacArthur is taking every precaution. Aircraft are being dispersed at Clark and Nichols Fields. All Army and Air Corps personnel are on full alert. Waiting for the other shoe to fall."

He paused yet again. "Although there is not yet an official state of war, we have received our orders from the Navy Department. They are explicit." He picked up a TOP SECRET dispatch and read.

EXECUTE UNRESTRICTED AIR AND SUBMARINE WAR-
FARE AGAINST JAPAN.

A somber hush fell over the room as the skippers
digested the momentous import of the dispatch. It meant
that, formal declaration or not, they were to wage war
against Japan. Not only that, they were to wage "unrestricted" submarine warfare. This meant that the London
Submarine Agreements of 1930, signed by the United
States, Great Britain and Japan, had been thrown out the
window. That treaty had placed severe limitations or
restrictions on the sinking of merchant vessels by submarines. Holmes recalled the key words of the treaty's Article
22: "A submarine may not sink or render incapable of
navigation a merchant vessel without having first placed
passengers, crew and ship's papers in a place of safety."
That is, in the lifeboats—a very risky operation for a
submarine.

Wilkes resumed. "I assume there is no doubt in
anyone's mind about the phrase 'unrestricted submarine
warfare'?"

"Sink the bastards on sight," Bart Bacon of *Pickerel*
said.

"*After* identity is established," Wilkes said. "Don't
sink neutral ships, for God's sake."

"Who the hell is neutral now?" Freddie Warder
demanded.

"We'll keep you informed on that," Wilkes said. He
went on. "If there is anyone with moral qualms about
conducting unrestricted submarine warfare, see me after
this meeting. You may request relief without prejudice."

There was not one man in the room who felt any
moral qualms; not after the sneak attack at Pearl Harbor.
Freddie Warder expressed it this way, "It's open season on
the slant-eyed, yellow bastards. And a good thing."

Wilkes went on. "At the conclusion of this meeting,
you will receive your operational orders. The submarine
war plan will become effective today at twelve hundred
hours. Noon. Eighteen boats—fourteen fleet boats, four S
boats—will leave for war patrol. Eleven boats will be held
in strategic reserve here in Manila Bay."

He then read off the names of the boats consigned to

the strategic reserve. *Swordray* was one of these. Holmes was furious. Wilkes knew damned well there was no finer boat than *Swordray*. But ever since Holmes had questioned the testing of the Mark Six magnetic exploder, Wilkes had been on his back. He had even chewed Holmes out for getting underway last night without prior permission. That *Swordray* was to be in the strategic reserve was deliberate punishment.

Along with half a dozen skippers, Holmes urgently raised his hand to protest, but Wilkes cut them off. "I am well aware that none of you wants to be in the reserve. But somebody has to do it and my decision is final. No requests for changes will be entertained."

The room was suddenly in uproar. Wilkes continued. "All right, knock it off. Pipe down. Here is your order of ship-sinking priority. One. Capital ships. Battlewagons, carriers, heavy and light cruisers. Give the tin cans a wide berth. You'll only get in trouble. Two. Loaded transports and troopships. Three. Light forces, transports and supply ships in ballast. Shoot on sight. One torpedo per merchant ship. Two at the most. Two per capital ship." He went on, reviewing instructions for practical use of the Mark Six magnetic torpedo exploder, emphasizing again that torpedoes should be set to run deep—thirty or forty feet.

He concluded with what Holmes thought was a strange rallying cry. "Now you men, listen to me. Don't go out there and try to win the Medal of Honor in a single day. Our submarines are our main striking force. Your crews are more valuable than anything else. *Bring them back.* Be cautious. Find out what you can about the enemy's anti-submarine forces for the benefit of all of us. Good luck and God speed."

Commander "Sunshine" Murray, Wilkes' tall operations officer, came into the room with a dark look on his usual cheerful face. He drew Wilkes aside for a brief conference. As Holmes watched from his seat, Wilkes appeared to pale. Then Wilkes again called for silence and said to the group, "Gentlemen, war has come to the Philippines. Ten minutes ago, Japanese aircraft bombed Clark Field. Damage reports are incomplete, as yet. But Admiral Hart reports that many of our planes were caught on the ground. At least half of MacArthur's air

force has been destroyed in a single stroke." He paused
and said, "I'm afraid we're in for a tough fight. Dis-
miss."

3

Swordray, like the other ten boats in the strategic reserve,
rode at anchor in Manila Bay, prepared to dive on an
instant's notice should Japanese aircraft appear over Manila.

Tom Bellinger pushed his way into the crew's mess, a
small area with four chrome tables and a galley in the
after battery compartment. The radio was tuned to a San
Francisco station. All men not on watch had crowded into
the mess to listen to President Roosevelt's address to
Congress. Through the crackling static, they heard the
familiar aristocractic voice: "Yesterday, December 7, 1941
—a date which will live in infamy—the United States was
suddenly and deliberately attacked by naval and air forces
of the Empire of Japan." As the crew listened in rapt
silence, Roosevelt went on to describe the attack in the
vaguest terms, concluding: "I ask that the Congress de-
clare that since the unprovoked and dastardly attack by
Japan on Sunday, December 7, 1941, a state of war has
existed between the United States and the Japanese Empire." The crew cheered Roosevelt's words. Now it was
official—reality.

So far, Bellinger thought, it has been a strange war.
Clark Field had been bombed. Half of MacArthur's
vaunted air force had been destroyed on the ground. (Just
why, after all the advance notice he had, no one knew. It
was scandalous.) But today, December 9 in Manila, the
Japanese had not followed up the attack. So far as Bellinger knew, there had been no bombing this day anywhere
in the Philippines. Why hadn't the Japanese tried to bomb
the ships and submarines in Manila Bay? *Holland*, for
instance? It was inexplicable.

The p.a. system barked, "Bellinger, lay up to the
wardroom. Bellinger . . ."

Bellinger made his way through the control room to

the forward battery and the wardroom. He found the captain, exec and the other three officers sitting around the table, still listening somberly to the radio. It was the exec who had summoned him. He had a classified document he wanted delivered to Sixteenth Naval District Branch in the Marsman Building.

"You want to make the trip yourself?" Phillips said with a knowing grin.

"Yes, sir," Bellinger said eagerly. He was happy enough for a chance to get ashore.

"Stay out of trouble," Phillips joked. "Don't do anything I wouldn't do."

Bellinger grinned, but he did not follow up with the usual trite repsonse. Instead he asked, "Any hurry on getting back?"

"No hurry," Phillips said. "Eighteen hundred?"

"Fine," Bellinger said. That would give him five hours on the beach. Fair enough.

Bellinger rode *Swordray*'s skiff to the fleet landing; Seaman Strong at the controls. Both men had heard the President's address to Congress.

"The shit's in the fan now," Strong said lugubriously.

"It sure is."

"I can't understand why they put us in this stupid reserve," Strong said. "We *know* they're coming. Why ain't we out there intercepting them?"

"You save your Sunday punch," Bellinger said. "When they find the Japs, they send us in." In fact, the reserve made no sense to Bellinger either. He deeply resented that they were in it.

"Stupid," Strong said, spitting.

"Have you communicated your views to Admiral Hart?" Bellinger said archly. "I'm sure he's dying to know what you think."

"Blow it out your ass."

Thereafter, they rode shoreward in silence, watching the ship traffic in the bay. All morning the merchant vessels had been getting up steam. Already most had fled southward toward Java—or beyond, to Australia. The bay was beginning to look deserted.

When they reached fleet landing, Bellinger climbed out and said, "Pick me up at seventeen-thirty."

"You lucky bastard," Strong said. "Hey. Get me a pint of gin, will you?"

"You can't take booze aboard a commissioned naval vessel," Bellinger admonished.

"I'll leave it in the skiff," Strong said. "She ain't commissioned. Come on, Tom." He offered Bellinger a small wad of crumpled, dirty pesos. Bellinger took the money and flagged a cab.

Manila seemed the same. Business as usual. Not a sign of war. At the Marsman Building, Bellinger debarked, told the driver to wait. Inside, he was pleased to find Navy personnel rushing about with an urgent, warlike air. He delivered the package to the proper place, got a signed receipt and returned to the cab.

Where to now? Bellinger was not certain. On impulse he said, "Rosaria's." He would make damned certain Rosaria had caught that Dutch ship. Otherwise, he would return her chest. It was a responsibility that was weighing heavily on him. Far more heavily than he had imagined.

When he rang the bell at Rosaria's, a strange face appeared at the open panel. Not Filipino, he noted. Chinese? Japanese? He gave his name. The face disappeared, the panel closed. He waited a full five minutes on the street before the door opened wide. And there stood the girl he knew as Maria, smiling enticingly.

"So, you're back," she said. "Come in."

"Is Rosaria here?" he asked carefully.

Maria's face clouded. "Rosaria is gone. Took ship to Singapore." She smiled again and added, "Under new management now. I am madam. Show you very good time. Two girls for price of one. And half Rosaria's prices."

Bellinger took this in without revealing the wave of uncertainty he inwardly felt. What was this, anyway? Maria had to have a patron, a backer. But who would lay out that kind of cash for a whorehouse in Manila on the brink of war?

Maria took Bellinger's arm in hers, brushing close. "Come," she said. "Very good time for you."

As much out of curiosity as anything else, Bellinger put aside his doubts and followed her inside. As they walked down the long stone passageway, she said, *"Swordray* not go on patrol?"

He said nothing and damned himself. His very presence ashore—here, anyway—gave away secrets.

"Are you making repairs?" she pressed.

"I told you before," he said evenly, "no questions."

She laughed and joked. "Big war. Boom. Boom. Military secrets." Then, seriously, "You remember I tell you Japanese will not come here?"

He remembered. "What about Clark Field?" he said.

"Defensive bombing," she said gravely. "The warmonger MacArthur was going to bomb Formosa. Those planes had to be destroyed. You'll see. The Philippines will remain neutral."

She led him into the patio. Nothing had changed. Except the girls. He did not recognize a single face. He was the only "client" in the place. "Bourbon, right?" she asked.

"Right."

She gave the order to a waiter in Chinese. Cantonese, he thought. Then she sat down and took his hand in hers. He moved his hand away and said, "What about Pearl Harbor?"

"Defensive," she said, smiling. "The fleet was going to attack Japan. Roosevelt had already given the order."

"Who told you that?"

"I heard it on the radio," she said. "A new program. An American on Radio Tokyo called Tokyo Rose. Very good music and news."

"Shit!" he snorted in disgust. He had heard one of Tokyo Rose's propaganda broadcasts. She was a traitor. And Maria—or whatever her real name was—had to be a spy. She had done her work, reaped her reward, and now, no doubt, she was gearing up for the Japanese brass to arrive. He'd better get out of here.

He watched as she signaled with her eyes to one of the girls at the next table. The girl rose and came over, slinking sexily along. She sat beside him and her hand went immediately to his crotch. She snuggled close, working her hand, murmuring some soft oriental sounds.

"That is Regina," Maria said, pulling her wicker chair closer to him. "Nice Eurasian girl from Hong Kong. Beautiful, no?"

"Your roommate at the convent?" he said sarcastically.

Her eyes widened in mock astonishment. "How did you know?"

"A birdie told me." He knew he should leave right then, but the girl was doing her work well. He was hard and her hand was working his buttons. It occurred to him that it would be a good idea to stay and find out what he could for Farland. All in the line of duty.

The three of them were soon naked in the big bed in Rosaria's old upstairs quarters. What ensued, Bellinger thought, was something akin to a work of art. He learned things he had never dreamed of before. He was just starting to relax when the door burst open and six SPs with levelled carbines stormed into the room shouting, "Reach," and, "Freeze." Bellinger instantly raised his arms over his head and edged off the bed to his feet, trembling all over and ashamed at his nakedness.

"Outside," one SP snapped at Maria and Regina. He pushed them out of the door. They were still stark naked.

"Who the hell are you?" the leading SP snarled at Bellinger.

Bellinger gave his name, rank, ship. He was more nervous than he had ever been in his life.

"What the fuck are you doing here?" the SP said. "This place is off limits."

"Since when?" Bellinger said. "I've been coming here for years."

"Since last week."

"I didn't know that," Bellinger said. "Do you mind if I get dressed?"

The SP nodded sullenly. Bellinger put on his uniform. Then the SP led him down to the patio, where a burly SP lieutenant was oveseeing the roundup and arrests of the girls. They were being shepherded out the front door into an SP paddy wagon. The lieutenant leveled a disgusted gaze at Bellinger. He said arrogantly, "Sailor, you're shit deep in trouble."

"I didn't know the place was off limits," Bellinger said. "There was no sign." He did not like this crew.

"I hear you been coming here for years," the lieutenant said, with real menace in his voice. "You know this is a Jap spy nest?"

"Yes," Bellinger said. "I was sure it was. I mean, lately. Since Rosaria left. I think the new madam, Maria, is a Jap spy."

"The one you were in bed with?" the lieutenant snarled.

"Yes," Bellinger conceded. *That* would take some explaining. He decided to say nothing more to the lieutenant. Farland would understand the need for additional research and clear him out of this.

"You're under arrest," the lieutenant said icily. "For suspected espionage."

Bellinger felt the blood drain from his face. If this charade went any further, he was going to cause the Old Man a lot of unnecessary trouble. He said, "Are you from O.N.I.?"

"What's that to you, sailor?" the lieutenant said.

"I've been working with O.N.I."

"Oh you have, have you. With who?" sneered the lieutenant, almost viciously.

"Chief Farland," Bellinger said. "I tipped him off about Maria. He said he would check her out."

"Chief Farland, eh?" the lieutenant echoed. "You picked a slim reed to lean on, sailor. Maybe on purpose, eh?"

"What do you mean, slim reed?" Bellinger asked.

"He was out at Clark Field yesterday," the lieutenant said. "He was killed in the first attack." He turned to one of the enlisted SPs. "Put the cuffs on him. Get him in the wagon."

4

In the *Swordray* wardroom, Phillips again glanced uneasily at the clock. 1910. Bellinger was now overdue by an hour and ten minutes. It was not like him to overstay a pass. There was something seriously wrong, Phillips decided. He confided his concern to Holmes, who was sitting at the head of the table, writing his daily letter home.

"Give him another hour," Holmes said, preoccupied with his letter. "Then send a party ashore to look for him."

Presently, the belowdecks watch messenger rapped on the bulkhead in the corridor. "Yes?" Phillips said.

"There's an SP launch alongside, sir," the messenger said, pulling the curtain open. "A Lieutenant Weller requests permission to come aboard to see the captain. I think it's about Bellinger, sir."

Phillips cast Holmes a long anxious look. "Send him below," Holmes said, capping his pen, pushing the tablet aside.

The messenger led Lieutenant Weller to the wardroom. Weller saluted, took off his cap and remained standing. Holmes introduced himself, then Phillips. He invited Weller to come and sit down.

"I'm afraid I've got some bad news about your quartermaster, Bellinger," Weller said, going straight to the point. "He's been arrested for suspected espionage."

"What!" Phillips almost shouted. "What the hell are you talking about?" He did not like the looks of this burly lieutenant. He had the air of a stupid bully.

"Go on," Holmes said calmly to Weller, concealing his astonishment. "Details, please."

"There's a place on Calle d'Oro called Rosaria's," Weller went on. "We've had it under close observation for ten days. A suspected spy nest. Since we put the surveillance in force, the place has been bought by a Filipino who is a known Jap spy. He re-staffed it with female personnel known to us, or strongly suspected by us, to be Jap spies. This afternoon, your Thomas Bellinger entered the premises —they're off limits—on unspecified business. We raided the place and put him under arrest."

Holmes and Phillips exchanged shocked glances. Holmes said, "I take it this Rosaria's is a whorehouse?"

"That's right," Weller said.

"And what evidence do you have that Bellinger was engaged in espionage?" Holmes said.

"What other business could he have had in an off-limits establishment?" Weller sneered.

"He could have gone there to get laid," Phillips said angrily. "What do most people go to whorehouses for? Hell, I *sent* him ashore on official business. He didn't ask to go ashore. For Christ's sake . . ."

"Hold on, George," Holmes interrupted, raising a calming hand. "I'll handle this." Then, to Weller, "You have proof of espionage?"

"It's circumstantial," Weller conceded, "but I think it is strong enough. Association, physical presence. He even admitted to me he believes that one of the girls we caught him in bed with was a Jap spy. You can't get much more intimate than that."

"He *told* you that?"

"Yes," Weller said. "I have a witness."

"Did he explain why he thought that?"

"No. He told us some cock-and-bull story about how he was working with O.N.I. With a man named Chief Farland. But, of course, Farland is dead. Killed at Clark Field yesterday. Nobody can check Bellinger's story. I'm sure he was well aware of Farland's death. The perfect cover story. If he *was* working with Farland—and I doubt it—it was possibly his intent to set himself up as a double agent."

"That is absolutely ridiculous," Holmes said finally. "I never knew a more dedicated, loyal sailor than Bellinger. And how in the world could he be a double agent when he's standing full-time watches on this ship?"

"They can be very clever," Weller said. "Very, very clever. He's been out here in Manila before, you know. Started in 1924 as a seaman, making eighteen bucks a month. Not much dough, even in those days. The Japs might have recruited him way back then. Paid him handsomely."

"He has no money!" Phillips said, fighting down a compelling urge to smack Weller in the face.

Weller spread his hands. "How do you know?"

"I *know!*" Phillips said, face white with rage.

"All the same," Weller said, "I'd like your permission to check his personal effects."

"By all means," Holmes said, glancing at Phillips.

"Sure," Phillips said. "I'm sure you won't find a damn thing."

"He has a locker?" Weller asked.

"Yes," Phillips said. "Come on, I'll show you."

They went aft to the crew's sleeping quarters located in the after battery, a dark air-conditioned space with thirty-six bunks in closely-mounted tiers. Word had spread through the crew. Those up and about stared at Weller with curiosity and open hostility. Phillips asked one of the men where Bellinger's locker was located. The man led them to it—port tier forward, bottom row, middle locker. It was padlocked.

They knocked the lock off with a small sledgehammer and chisel. The racket woke everyone in the compartment. Those awakened were not happy and let it be known.

Kneeling on the deck, Weller probed the locker, pulling out socks, shaving kit, skivvies, then with a grunt, the heavy, ornate teak box wrapped in a sheet. He removed the sheet, examined the chest and said, "Let's take this back to the wardroom."

Phillips led the way back with a mounting apprehension, allowing Weller to struggle with the heavy chest. Weller set it down on the wardroom table. Then, as Holmes and Phillips looked on with growing dread, he knocked the lock off with the sledge. He raised the lid. The top compartment of the chest was crammed with little chamois bags with drawstrings. He opened one bag and dumped the contents on the table. Out poured two or three dozen large, high-grade diamonds. Holmes and Phillips turned ashen-faced and sat down heavily while Weller closely examined the diamonds.

"No money, eh?" Weller said. "I'd say this ice was worth four or five grand." He dumped the rest of the bags on the table. Out flowed emeralds, rubies, pearls, jade, sapphires. Holmes and Phillips stared in disbelief.

"He did all right for a first class petty officer," Weller said smugly, lifting the tray.

They saw that the lower portion of the chest was brim-full of Filipino fifty-dollar gold coins. Weller ran his hands through the coins like a pirate, whistling low and long. Then he said, "Well, I'll take this evidence down to headquarters and . . ."

"Like hell you will," Holmes snapped. "That chest doesn't leave this ship."

"But regulations . . ."

"Screw your regulations," Holmes said. "If you think I'm turning this treasure over to *you*, you've got another think coming."

"I'll go to the admiral," Weller said.

"Go to the admiral," Holmes said. "When the admiral orders me to turn this over to you, I will. Not before."

"Then I'll need a signed inventory from you," Weller said.

"A signed inventory you can have," Holmes said. "Nothing more."

The three of them divided the contents of the chest, counted their individual piles and then prepared an inventory. There were forty thousand dollars in gold coins. Weller estimated the "ice" was worth another ten thousand. Holmes, shocked dumb, signed the inventory in quadruplicate, keeping one copy (countersigned by Phillips and Weller) for himself. Then he put the chest in the safe in his cabin.

When Phillips finally found his voice, he was still firmly convinced of Bellinger's innocence. "There must be some logical explanation for this."

"I'd sure like to hear it," Weller said. "I bet it'll be a beaut." He was immensely pleased at his gumshoe work. "Well, thanks for your help, gentlemen. If not before, see you in court."

He put on his cap and started out.

"Where is Bellinger?" Phillips said.

"Cavite brig," Weller said. "Sixteenth Naval District Headquarters."

"He'll need a defense lawyer," Phillips said. "Can we see him?"

"Oh, sure," Weller said. "Check in with Lieutenant Commander MacIntosh."

"MacIntosh," Phillips repeated.

When Weller had gone, Phillips sighed deeply and said to Holmes, "This is crazy. I still say there's some other explanation. I'd bet my bottom dollar Tom Bellinger is no spy."

"The whole thing's crazy," Holmes said. "And I don't like that Weller's looks."

5

Tom Bellinger paced the tiny, dank cell in near-panic. Farland was dead! They would search his locker. Who would believe him? Goddamn it to hell! Why hadn't he followed his better instincts and gotten out of there? He smacked his fist into his hand, kicked the thick stone wall as hard as he could.

He became aware of footsteps in the passageway, then a heavy key sliding into the lock of the solid steel door. The door opened, the passageway light fanned across the cell deck. A guard stood aside. The Old Man walked into the cell carrying a white, lined tablet. Thank God for a familiar face!

"Well, Bellinger," Holmes said, "what the hell is going on?"

"I'm being railroaded," Bellinger blurted out. "These people are crazy. I'm not a spy."

"We found the chest," Holmes said. The guard remained standing by the open door.

"I can explain that," Bellinger said. "It's not mine. I'm keeping it for a friend."

Holmes sat down on the bunk watching Bellinger pace for a moment. Then he took out his pen and said, "Suppose you start from the beginning."

Bellinger began at the beginning, 1925, when he had first met Rosaria. He told how he and Jack Lyons had recently looked up Rosaria. (That could be verified.) Then he told of his suspicions about "Maria," his visit to Farland at O.N.I., (that, too, could be verified in the sign-in log), Rosaria's panicky eleventh-hour sale of the establishment, her request that he keep her valuables, her departure on the S.S. *Piet Heyn* (that could also be verified), and the details of his impulsive visit that afternoon, to make damn sure Rosaria had actually left.

Holmes jotted the salient points of the narrative on the tablet, filling three full pages.

"That's all there is to it, Captain," Bellinger concluded, wearily sitting down on a footstool.

Holmes stared long and hard at his quartermaster. His story was logical, convincing, partly verifiable. Except, Holmes felt, for one angle. Why would a whore—a shrewd madam—entrust her life's savings to a sailor she might never see again? He put the question to Bellinger.

"We're old, old friends," Bellinger said. "As I told you, we go way, way back. I guess I am the only person she felt she could trust."

Holmes tried to digest—and accept—this statement. He knew, of course, that enlisted men formed close friendships with the whores. In some cases, they married them.

"It's a lot of money," he said.

"She was in a panic, sir," Bellinger said. "She was running. She was right, as it turned out. And she was right about carrying all that dough around. I'm sure someone would have knocked her off."

"She wasn't part of it, was she?" Holmes asked. "Not a spy?"

"Oh, hell no, sir," Bellinger said. "If so, why should she run?"

"There could have been a problem we don't know about," Holmes said.

"No, sir," Bellinger said firmly. "She's no more a spy than I am." He was silent for a moment, then, "Sir, do you believe me?"

"I believe you," Holmes said.

"I'm sorry as hell about this, Captain," Bellinger said. "I didn't mean to cause you this headache."

"Well, as I see it," Holmes said, "when you went to Farland, you were acting in the best interest of the naval establishment. You're to be commended—not condemned. You spun a web, but unfortunately, you got caught in it." He rose. "Never mind about the headache, Bellinger. That's what skippers are for. Now don't worry. I'll do everything I can to get you out of here."

6

By the time Seaman Strong brought the skiff alongside *Holland*, it was almost 2000 hours. Holmes climbed out and said, "Wait here for me. I shouldn't be long."

"Aye, aye, Captain," Strong said. He watched Holmes mount the gangway to the quarterdeck. He knew the reason for this late night visit. They all did. Strong crossed his fingers.

Holmes saluted the quarterdeck watch officer and proceeded directly to the office of Commodore John Wilkes. Even though it was late, he noted that the whole staff seemed to be up and rushing about urgently. He knocked on the closed door labeled "Commander, Submarines, Asiatic Fleet," and entered to find Wilkes, his chief of staff James Fife, the operations officer "Sunshine" Murray and others huddled around a desk.

Wilkes looked up as if annoyed by the interruption. "What do you want, Holmes?" he said coldly.

"Sir," Holmes said. "I've got an urgent personnel problem I'd like to discuss. . . ."

"Personnel problem!" Wilkes echoed. "See the personnel officer."

"It's not that, sir," Holmes said. "One of my men is in the Cavite brig."

"For Christ's sake, Holmes," Wilkes said. "Don't you know there's a war on? We're busy trying to re-deploy a submarine force. Handle your own personnel problems."

"Re-deploy?" Holmes asked.

"Yes," Wilkes said. "The admiral's given up on Mac-Arthur. He can't provide us air support. We're moving *Holland* south—to Java. We're setting up our headquarters ashore. And *Swordray* leaves for patrol tomorrow. I'm committing the whole reserve force. . . ."

"Sir!" Holmes said, interrupting. "My quartermaster, Bellinger, has been charged with suspected espionage."

"Espionage!" Wilkes cried, eyes widening.

"Yes, sir," Holmes replied. He gave Wilkes a summary version of what had happened, concluding with his own opinion, "He's been railroaded."

"Goddammit!" Wilkes suddenly exploded. "I don't have time for this, Holmes. Your men are *your* responsibility. I've got a war to fight."

"But, sir," Holmes pleaded. "We can't throw this innocent man to those O.N.I. wolves. I need that man to run my ship. Would you please . . . ?"

Wilkes was furious. He jumped up and shouted, "Get out! Get out of here or I'll relieve you of command on the spot!"

7

Tom Bellinger sat despondently on his bunk in the Cavite brig, smoking his last cigarette. It was almost noon. He had heard nothing from the captain—or anybody else.

He heard the key turn in the slot. A guard admitted Lieutenant Weller and two yeomen. Weller opened his attaché case and said without ceremony, "We want an official statement from you, Bellinger. And no bullshit."

Bellinger stared hard at Weller, fighting down an urge to strangle him. The two yeomen sat on the bunk, pens poised on yellow legal pads.

"Okay," Weller said. "Full name, serial number, date of initial enlistment and dates of re-enlistment."

Bellinger forced himself to calm down. It would do him no good to be hostile. He started pacing and answering the questions put to him.

Ten minutes into the interview, they heard the Cavite air-raid siren moan, then shouts of "Take cover" in the passageway. Then the dull thump-thump of the three-inch anti-aircraft guns.

Weller broke off his questions and dashed out into the passageway. He returned a moment later and said to his yeomen, "Jap bombers. Let's get the hell to the shelter."

They left Bellinger in the cell, the door ajar. A moment later a bomb fell on the brig. The force of it blew the heavy steel door off its hinges and hurtled Bellinger into the passageway. Stunned, he got to his knees, then to his feet. Searing flames shot down the passageway. He ran through the flames to the orderly room door. He yanked open the door and found himself looking into open space. The orderly room was gone. Bombs were erupting all over the base. He saw one hit the paint shop, another the torpedo repair shop then another the mess hall. All three buildings were blown to pieces. In seconds, it seemed, Cavite was an inferno of flames and deafening explosions.

Bellinger could see the bombers—silvery glints very high in the sky. Far beneath them he saw the puffs of black smoke from the flak. There was no way the guns could reach those high-flying bombers. Nor were there any interceptors in evidence. Cavite was defenseless.

Bellinger climbed over the stone rubble that had been the orderly room to get to the street. There he found Weller and the two yeomen, lying facedown, covered with blood. Weller and one yeoman were dead, but the other yeoman—the skinny one—was breathing weakly. Bellinger slung the yeoman over his shoulder, stooped to pick up Weller's attaché case, and ran through the inferno for the base hospital.

The hospital had not been hit—yet. Its entry was jammed with wounded crying aloud in pain. Bellinger propped the yeoman against the wall and waited until a corpsman got to him. Then he ran for the air-raid shelter he had passed up the street. It, too, was jammed, but the men made a place for him.

In a half hour it was all over. The high-flying planes went away. Emergency crews of every kind deployed into the ravaged streets, picking up the dead and wounded or putting out the raging fires. Cavite was a complete shambles. Hundreds must be dead or dying.

Bellinger sat on the running board of a demolished truck to consider what he should do. He opened the briefcase. In addition to the yeomen's yellow pads with the notes, it contained what appeared to be the complete file on Bellinger's "spy case." He leafed through the documents, finding nothing new or surprising. Then he got up and threw the entire contents of the briefcase into a burning building. He watched as the papers were consumed. With Weller dead, the file destroyed and the

Sixteenth Naval Headquarters in ruins, it would be hard
—if not impossible—for the Navy to pursue the case
against him. To all intents, he was a free man again. He
would return to *Swordray* and resume his duties as though
Weller and the "case" had never existed.

He walked out the unguarded main gate of Cavite
and hitchhiked to Manila.

8

In the *Swordray* wardroom, Phillips reported to Holmes,
"Ready in all respects for sea, Captain."

"Good work, George," Holmes said, folding and
inserting the letter to Helen in an envelope. The prepara-
tion for getting underway had been delayed by the bombing attack on Cavite. *Swordray* and the other boats had
submerged in the bay during the attack.

"The word from Cavite is bad," Phillips went on.
"The place is a total shambles. Hundreds dead. Nearly
three hundred torpedoes were blown up. They got *Sealion*
and nearly got *Seadragon*." He paused a moment, then
said, "I hope Bellinger's all right."

"Yes," Holmes said. "We've got to do something to
get him cleared of that ridiculous charge. I'll go see the
Admiral as soon as we get back. I wish to God we had
more time now. We'll have to rearrange the watch sched-
ules to get someone else to take over Bellinger's duties."

"That's no problem for one patrol, sir. We can make
do just fine for a short time, but I sure wouldn't want to
fight the rest of the war without him. I just hope he wasn't
injured in the bombing raid." He stopped speaking, cleared
his throat and changed the subject. "Captain, I'd like
permission to go ashore for two hours."

Holmes looked at the clock. It was 1300. They had
orders to get underway for patrol at 1500. Holmes smiled
knowingly at his exec, handed him the letter and said,
"While you're there, mail this for me, will you?"

"Sure," Phillips said eagerly. He put the letter in his
tunic.

"Tell her goodbye for me," Holmes added.

Forewarned, Seaman Strong had the skiff ready, motor idling. Phillips climbed aboard and they headed for fleet landing. At exactly 1310, while they were still offshore, the high-flying bombers appeared over Manila and went to work. They heard the distant explosions, then saw the fire and smoke rising above the city. There were no interceptors; the three-inch anti-aircraft guns could not reach the bombers' altitude.

"Bastards!" Strong hissed between clenched teeth. He throttled the motor back and circled the skiff.

Phillips nodded silently, watching the silvery glints wheeling high in the sky. They seemed to be working over the military installations and the railroad yards, not the residential areas. Anne was safe for now—but for how much longer? The planes bombed at will for a half hour, then, precisely at 1340, they formed up and disappeared to the north. When they were out of sight, Strong guided the skiff to the landing.

As luck would have it, Phillips spotted a grey Navy car, bearing the insignia "ComSubRon 2," parked near the landing. It was Red Doyle's car, apparently overlooked and left behind in *Holland*'s hasty departure. The key was in the ignition. Phillips climbed behind the wheel, started the engine and drove off

Manila was a different city now. The streets were jammed with military vehicles of every description. The shop windows were boarded up, the government buildings and banks and hotels were sandbagged. Squads of Filipino soldiers patrolled the sidewalks; MPs directed traffic on the main streets and boulevards. Military and civilian ambulances and fire trucks tore through the city, sirens screaming.

Phillips parked the car in front of the High Commissioner's mansion. It, too, was now heavily sandbagged. A platoon of Marines was bivouacked on the lawn.

He found Anne Simpson in her second floor office, staring at her typewriter, fingers poised over the keyboard, lost in thought. When she saw him, her face lit up and she cried out happily, "George! I thought you were gone!"

She jumped up and ran into his arms. They kissed

hungrily, passionately, holding one another close. Phillips kicked the door shut behind him. Finally Anne broke away and said, "I was afraid you'd leave without my seeing you. When are you going?"

"Today," he said. "In a few minutes." She sat on the corner of her desk, not taking her eyes from his. "Anne," he continued, "the Japs landed at Vigan today. It's just a matter of time. You've got to get out of Manila."

"Why is the Navy so defeatist?" Anne said.

"Not defeatist," he said. "Realistic. Anne, MacArthur's air power is *gone*. You can't win without air power."

"Help is on the way."

"No it isn't."

"A convoy," she insisted.

"The *Pensacola* convoy?"

"Yes."

"It's been diverted to Australia," he said.

"What? Why?"

"It can't get here," he said. "It would be slaughtered by Jap air. Anne, listen to me, please. *We have no air power*. That is the reality. And that's why you have to get out of here."

"What about the submarines?"

"We'll do all we can," he said, "but Cavite's gone. *Holland*'s gone. We don't have any backup facilities. So I'm not sure how effective we can be. Look, will you face it? You've *got* to get out of here while you can."

She sighed deeply and said, "I can't leave, George. I have a job to do."

"They'll level Manila like they did Cavite," he said. "Then they'll invade. Is your work *that* vital?"

"London withstood the blitz," she said. "So can we."

"The Germans didn't *invade* England."

"All the same, I can't leave. Anyway, there's no way to leave now. No more transportation out."

"Marry me and you'll be a Navy dependent," he said. "The Navy'll find transportation for you."

"No," she said. "I won't do it that way. That's not . . . not right. I could never live with myself."

"Anne! This is war, dammit. You seize *any* expedient."

"Not I."

"The Japs don't take prisoners," he said. "It could be . . . horrible."

She shrugged and changed the subject. "How long will you be gone?"

"I'm not sure," he said. "Two, three weeks. It depends."

She opened the desk drawer and took out a sealed package. "It's a photograph," she said. "I had it done for you last week. To help you remember."

"That's nice of you," he said, "but I don't think I'll forget."

"I know you sailors," she winked. "New port. New girl."

"Anne! You promised you wouldn't say that again."

"Just kidding." She stood up and held him close. "Oh, God! This is so hard. I love you, George. You know that. I'll miss you dreadfully. But don't worry about me. I'll be fine. I'll be right here when you get back. You just take care of yourself, and come back safely to me."

9

It took Tom Bellinger four separate rides to get from Cavite to Manila. The last was an Army six-by-six truck loaded with food stores. The driver was a U.S. Army sergeant, chewing on a dead cigar butt.

"Jump in, Mac" the sergeant said, looking at Bellinger's filthy, bloodstained uniform.

Bellinger climbed into the cab and lit a cigaret, hands shaking. The sergeant said, "Many people hurt?"

"Hundreds," Bellinger said grimly. He could still hear the screams of the dying.

"They hit Nichols Field, too," the sergeant said. "Wiped it out."

"I didn't see a single interceptor up there," Bellinger said.

"There are no more interceptors," the sergeant said. "The Air Corps is gone. Kaput." He lit the cigar butt and went on. "The Japs landed up on the north coast today. Place called Aparri. You know that place?"

"No," Bellinger said. "We just got out here a couple of weeks ago."

"A diversion, I think," the sergeant said. "The main force will land in Lingayen Gulf, then head straight for Manila. The land is flat, good for tanks."

The sergeant, a compulsive talker, outlined the complete defensive strategy of the Northern Force, the Filipino troops assigned to stop the Japs. He concluded his account in a sarcastic tone. "That's the so-called plan. It's a joke. The Filipino's can't fight, don't even *want* to fight, and they ain't got nothing to fight *with*. A few light tanks, some artillery, and World War I Enfield rifles. The minute the Japs land in force, they'll bug out. Where you going anyway, Mac?"

"Fleet landing," Bellinger said.

"I'll drop you off."

"I can make it from here," Bellinger said.

"No trouble," the sergeant insisted, grinding down through the gears, skillfully threading through the teeming streets.

When Bellinger reached fleet landing, he saw that Manila Bay was virtually empty of ships. *Holland* was nowhere in sight, nor were the reserve submarines. It was 1600. *Swordray* had sailed an hour before.

Chapter Five

1

The watch messenger delivered another radio message to Holmes in the wardroom. Holmes read:

YOUR ORDERS PATROL CAMRANH BAY CANCELLED. NEW PATROL STATION SOUTHERN APPROACHES HAINAN ISLAND. WATCH FOR MAIN LUZON INVASION FORCES. WILKES.

Holmes scowled and passed the message to Phillips. Phillips scanned it and exploded. "Goddammit! They must all be crazy."

It was the fourth change of patrol station for *Swordray* in as many days. The original sealed orders instructed them to patrol off Formosa. En route, they were shifted to Hong Kong. Then to Camranh Bay, Indochina, now Hainan Island. The other Asiatic Fleet boats were also being shifted around willy-nilly. None had yet found any sign of the main Luzon invasion forces, or any other targets of note. The seas appeared to be empty of Japanese maritime forces.

Phillips fumed on, "They're not going to stage an invasion from Hainan. It'll come from Formosa, or the Pescadores. That's as plain as the nose on your face."

Holmes had to agree. The original orders to patrol Formosan waters made sense. The invasion force would certainly come from the north. It would almost certainly land at Lingayen Gulf. But, inexplicably, Wilkes had only one boat patrolling the gulf, the ancient *S-36*. The fleet boats were scattered all over the South China Sea. It was stupid beyond belief. And, Holmes thought, the new orders for *Swordray* to patrol Hainan went beyond stupidity. It was as though Wilkes were deliberately punishing *Swordray* again.

He concealed his disgust. "Ours is not to reason why," he said airily. "Give me a new course."

Phillips had it ready. "Zero zero four, Captain."

Holmes went to the bridge. Henry Slack had the deck, the four-to-eight watch. It was a fine tropical evening. Bright moon, calm sea. The world was now totally engulfed in war, but here it seemed very far away.

"Evening, Hank," Holmes said. "They've changed our orders again. This time it's Hainan Island."

"For God's sake," Slack said with a weary sigh. "Can't they make up their minds?"

"Your new course is zero zero four," Holmes said.

"Aye, sir." Slack spoke into the bridge intercom. "Come right to zero zero four."

The helmsman in the conning tower below repeated the order, then said, "Steady on zero zero four."

"Very well," Slack said, looking aft at the wide turn in the wake.

"Permission to come on the bridge?" the intercom spoke. It was Quartermaster Second Class Les Reed who had replaced Tom Bellinger as assistant navigator and taken over the gang.

"Granted," Slack said.

Reed came up through the hatch, binoculars slung from his neck. He was a six-year man who had shipped over in Pearl Harbor. He had been listening to a gloomy news broadcast on the radio. He said to Holmes and Slack, "They sank the *Prince of Wales* and *Repulse*."

"What?" Holmes exclaimed. "How?"

"Dive bombers," Reed said.

"My God," Holmes said, thoroughly shaken. The principal capital ships of the proposed combined Asiatic Fleet were gone. That left the heavy cruiser *Houston* as the number one ship.

"They were trying to intercept the Japanese invasion

forces headed for Malaya," Reed elaborated. "Hong Kong and Wake are still holding out."

"Any news of Manila?" Holmes asked.

"Heavy bombing," Reed said. "No word on the main invasion force."

All three men fell silent for a time, digesting the bad news. The Japs could do no wrong, it seemed. One audacious stroke after the other. The whole Pacific and Far East going under, bit by bit.

The silence was interrupted by an electrifying cry from a lookout in his cage high in the periscope shears. "Ship dead ahead!"

Holmes, Slack and Reed raised their binoculars as one, focusing dead ahead. Holmes felt a momentary wave of apprehension. It was his and *Swordray*'s first contact with the enemy. They were alone, deep in Japanese waters. The outcome of the encounter would depend to a very great extent on his judgment, skill and resourcefulness. All that he had learned in fifteen long years of naval service was about to be put to the ultimate test.

"Think it's a tin can," the lookout added. Then, "It *is* a tin can, sir. Headed right for us."

Holmes could now make out the ship's distant top hamper and the peeling phosphorescent bow wave. He estimated the range at ten thousand yards. Five miles. With a combined closing speed of forty knots, he calculated, they would be nose to nose in about seven or eight minutes. He said to Slack, "Go to battle stations."

"Battle stations, aye," Slack echoed immediately, pulling the bridge alarm.

Les Reed watched the onrushing destroyer, transfixed with hypnotic dread. So this was the enemy! Two or three hundred Japanese sailors inside those steel plates, trained to find and kill submarines.

The intercom crackled tersely, "All hands at battle stations." It was George Phillips in the conning tower.

Holmes said, "Very well, George. We've got a tin can up here. He's probably in the van of a convoy. We'll let him go by and see what's behind him."

Holmes was surprised at his own calmness. The tin can was not an American ship out to give *Swordray* a torpedo drill. She was the enemy. Deadly and unforgiving. *Swordray* could not make one mistake.

He watched the destroyer in his binoculars for another full minute. It was coming on fast, growing ever larger and more menacing. The intercom broke into his thoughts. "Captain, we track the ship on base course one eight zero, speed twenty-eight. She's zig-zagging radically."

"Very well," Holmes said with satisfaction. His initial speed estimate had been right on the button. He turned to Slack, "Okay, Hank, let's pull the cork."

Holmes ducked down the hatch to the conning tower as Slack cried, "Clear the bridge! Clear the bridge! Dive! Dive!" He simultaneously rang the diving alarm. The Klaxon *auuugahed* twice throughout the boat. The diesels shut down, the great main engine air induction thudded shut, the ballast tank vents clanked open and *Swordray* nosed down.

Reed and the two lookouts preceded Slack down the hatch to the conning tower, now crowded with battle station personnel. When Slack came down, he grabbed the hatch lanyard and pulled it shut. Reed stepped up, turned the wheel and dogged it tight.

"Green board, pressure in the boat," Jack Lyons shouted from his station in the control room. They heard the hiss of the high-pressure air bleeding into the boat.

"Very well," Slack said, eye on the depth gauge. *Swordray* was going past forty feet. He shouted to Lyons, "Make your depth sixty feet."

"High speed screws dead ahead," the sonar operator said, adjusting his padded earphones. He sat on a stool at the sonar stack in the rear of the conning tower.

Swordray, propelled by her giant 250-cell battery, was eerily quiet. Even the men lowered their voices when giving or acknowledging orders. She went down, down into her silent world.

"Sixty feet," Lyons reported. The boat leveled off, rock steady.

"Up scope," Holmes said.

Reed pushed the button to start the periscope hoist motor. As the scope came up, Holmes squatted and grabbed the folded handles, snapped them in place and jammed his right eye into the molded-rubber socket. "There she is," he said. "Mark!"

The destroyer was now less than a half-mile away, coming dead on at high speed. She was a sitting duck. But Wilke's orders were to avoid destroyers. If they attacked her, she would alert the convoy behind her and *Swordray* would lose one of her most priceless battle assets: surprise.

"Down scope," Holmes said.

Reed lowered the scope. They could now hear the high-speed screws through the hull. They stood in silence as the destroyer thundered overhead. Then Holmes said to the sonarman, "Forget the tin can. Keep your gear dead ahead."

They waited patiently for twenty minutes, smoking and chatting in low voices, speculating on whether the tin can was alone or escorting a convoy. The sonarman answered the question. "Low-speed screws dead ahead." It was a convoy.

"Up scope."

Holmes searched dead ahead. The moon was very bright, well past its zenith and now in the west. His eye caught a distant shape. A ship. Then another and another. "A large convoy," he said. "Stand by! Mark!"

Reed read off the bearing, relaying it to the tracking party and the torpedo data computer (TDC) operator, engineering officer Fred Bohlen. Holmes estimated the range of the ship with the periscope stadimeter, guessing at the masthead height when he split the image. He could accurately estimate warship masthead heights but he was not accustomed to merchant ships. That was going to require considerable experience before they got it down pat.

The convoy lumbered on toward them. Holmes maneuvered *Swordray* slightly eastward so the formation of ships would be "down moon"—the moon behind the convoy. He set up on the lead ship, a heavily-laden freighter with a deckload of knocked-down Zero fighters. As ordered by Wilkes, he would fire one torpedo from very close range to run at a depth of thirty feet. Ignited by the magnetic exploder, the torpedo would instantly break the freighter's back.

They solved the fire control problem quickly and efficiently. Holmes said, "Make ready tube number one. Open the outer door."

"Number one ready. Outer door open."

"Fire one!" Holmes said, eye in the periscope.

They felt the jolt as compressed air catapulted the torpedo from the forward tube. Holmes kept the periscope up to watch the torpedo run. He could see its steamy wake plainly in the moonlight. He reported, "Running hot, straight and normal. Looks like a perfect shot."

Again he was surprised at his calmness. And pleased. He had trained hard in peacetime to control his emotions in torpedo drills, keeping talk at a minimum. But he was never sure this calmness would obtain during the real thing.

"Thirty seconds," Reed intoned, eyes fixed on the stop watch. The calculated torpedo run at this close range was thirty-six seconds. Holmes could see the torpedo wake, converging on the track of the ship. It was indeed a perfect shot. The torpedo would run under the ship directly beneath the midships bridge structure. There was no sign the torpedo had been seen, the convoy alerted.

"Thirty-six seconds," Reed intoned.

Holmes' eye was riveted on the target, waiting for it to explode in flames. But nothing happened.

"Forty seconds."

Still nothing happened.

George Phillips looked at the stop watch in dismay. What the hell was going on? It had been *the* perfect approach.

"It's a miss," Holmes finally said at the periscope. "I don't see how, but we missed."

"Goddammit!" Phillips said, voicing the towering disappointment they all felt.

"A perfect setup," Holmes said. "Absolutely textbook. Well, they're none the wiser. Let's get the next ship in line."

They set up on the next ship, moved in even closer and fired number two tube. The torpedo run was again perfect. But, again, nothing happened.

"Another miss," Holmes finally conceded in a bitter

tone. "What the hell's the matter with us? All right, gang. We'll try again. New setup. Stand by! Mark!"

They very carefully set up on the third target, moving in so close—seven hundred yards—Holmes felt he could reach out and touch the ship. This time they stretched their orders a hair and fired two torpedoes, ten seconds apart, one to hit the bow, one to hit the stern. Both torpedoes ran exactly as aimed. But, again, there was no explosion.

"Four fish, four misses," Holmes said with utmost disgust. "What the hell are we doing wrong?"

He returned to the periscope. Most of the convoy had passed them by, but he found a straggler limping slowly behind the main formation. It was a big freighter. "Make ready tubes five and six," he said. "Stand by! Mark!"

They closed to point-blank range—five hundred yards —and set up and fired two more torpedoes. The short torpedo runs were perfect. But again, nothing happened. They had fired six torpedoes at four targets in almost laboratory-like conditions with no explosions. What the hell *was* going on?

Utterly discouraged, Holmes blamed himself. Somehow he had erred. Perhaps in the masthead height or the speed estimates. But how could that be? The torpedo runs could not have been better. Was there something wrong with his eyesight? He ordered the forward tubes reloaded.

"Captain, I think I've got more heavy screws at zero zero zero," the sonarman reported.

"Up scope," Holmes said.

He soon confirmed the report. A second large convoy was following hard on the heels of the first. Holmes let the lead escort go by then he set up on the first ship in the near column. He stepped back from the periscope and said, "George, maybe there's something wrong with my eyes. You take the scope."

The two men switched places. Phillips manned the scope, working the stadimeter, putting the cross hairs on the target's midship bridge. They again closed to point-blank range and fired two torpedoes. Both ran perfectly. Neither exploded.

"Eight misses!" Phillips snarled. "It's not possible!

There must be something radically wrong with those torpedoes, Captain."

"It *could* be that," Holmes said, nodding, lost in thought.

"Maybe they are running deeper than they're supposed to," Phillips went on. "Maybe they're running *beneath* the magnetic field of the ship and the exploder is *not* being activated."

"That's a possibility," Holmes said. "All right. We'll do it. Let's see if you're right. Set three and four to run at twenty feet."

Holmes took the periscope back and set up on the next target, a big tanker. They fired both torpedoes set to run at a depth of twenty feet. The torpedo runs were again perfect. But there were no explosions.

"I give up," Holmes said to Phillips. "Take the scope."

"Let's try ten feet," Phillips said, putting his eye into the periscope socket. "Here's a troop transport."

"All right," Holmes said with a deep sigh of resignation. "Set five and six to run at ten feet."

Phillips conducted a cool, skilled approach, taking his time, obtaining repeated bearings. Again they fired from point-blank range. Phillips watched the two wakes streaking at the ship and said, "Running hot, straight, and normal, Captain."

The words were scarcely out of his mouth when *Swordray* was rocked by an awesome explosion. The force of it threw them against the conning tower bulkhead. Phillips scrambled back to the periscope and shouted, "A hit! She's sinking, Captain."

He stepped away from the scope. Holmes took it over and put the cross hairs on the stricken transport. She was down by the bow and afire amidships. He could see frantic activity on her decks. Sailors and soldiers rushing around madly, scores of them leaping over the rails into the sea. He observed the panic with a blood-thirsty joy that astonished him. He hoped there would not be a single survivor. As the ship plunged under the sea, he stepped away from the scope, picked up the p.a. mike and said, "Scratch one of the Emperor's transports."

A resounding cheer could be heard all through

Swordray. But neither Holmes nor Phillips joined in the victory celebration. They had fired half their torpedoes—twelve of twenty-four—to sink one ship. They had disobeyed strictest orders about the depth setting to achieve the sinking. There was going to be hell to pay.

2

Swordray patrolled the south coast of Hainan Island for the next week. They saw nothing—not even a sampan. Holmes, Phillips and the torpedo data computer operator Fred Bohlen utilized the time to analyze in minute detail the twelve torpedo shots, re-creating on paper each shot with the firing data from Les Reed's log book. The analysis convinced them that their initial instinct was correct: the torpedoes appeared to be running deeper than designed.

On the evening of the seventh day, they surfaced after dark, set up a battery charge and manned the assigned radio frequency. This night it was flooded with encoded messages to and from Wilkes and his submarines.

The first was from Ray Lamb's *Stingray* which had relieved the old *S-36* at Lingayen Gulf. It was the long-awaited contact report:

ENEMY INVASION FORCE EIGHTY TRANSPORTS STANDING INTO LINGAYEN GULF.

Wilkes replied tersely:

PENETRATE GULF. ATTACK. ATTACK. ATTACK.

But Lamb came back:

UNABLE PENETRATE GULF DUE LEAKS. REQUEST PERMISSION RETURN TO MANILA FOR REPAIRS.

Holmes read the radio traffic with mounting dismay and disbelief. Why hadn't Wilkes deployed more boats at Lingayen Gulf? What was wrong with Ray Lamb? Why hadn't he attacked the invasion force? And why, at a critical time like this, would he request permission to return to Manila to repair leaks? That would leave the gulf completely unguarded.

The next several messages were from Wilkes. He ordered *Stingray* to return to Manila. At the same time, he ordered six boats—*S-38, S-40, Salmon, Saury, Permit* and *Porpoise*—to converge on Lingayen Gulf, penetrate and attack the invasion forces. Studying the messages, Phillips, too, was dismayed. "It's too late," he said to Holmes. "They've already landed."

Holmes nodded. "They'll throw a destroyer screen across the mouth of the gulf. No one will be able to get inside."

"Closing the barn door after the horses have gone," Phillips said grimly.

His thoughts were less on Lingayen Gulf than on Manila and Anne Simpson. Manila had been bombed every day since they left. The heavily-censored news dispatches gave no specifics. Nor was High Commissioner Sayre ever mentioned. Only General MacArthur and his pompous, egotistical and propagandistic references to "my Air Force," or "my troops," or "my Navy."

The wardroom radio was tuned to Tokyo. Phillips was half-listening when Tokyo Rose interrupted the music for a "news report."

"Attention American sailors and soldiers," she said in her dulcet tone. "Today the illustrious Japanese General Masaharu Homma landed his troops in two places on the island of Luzon in the Philippines: Lingayen Gulf and Lamon Bay. The landings were unopposed. Filipino troops threw down their weapons and fled into the hills. The Eleventh and Seventy-first Filipino Divisions of the North Luzon Force have ceased to exist as military units. The victorious Japanese troops are marching on Manila from two directions while General MacArthur languishes in his Manila Hotel penthouse. American soldiers and sailors! Further resistance is futile. You have lost the war. Lay down your arms so that you will live to see your loved ones again."

Phillips did not doubt the truth of the broadcast. *Stingray* had already confirmed the landing at Lingayen Gulf. Manila, situated between Lingayen Gulf and Lamon Bay, was now caught in giant pincers. MacArthur's lightly-armed conscript army faced Japan's China-hardened regular army shock troops toughened by years of fighting in China. The Japanese had air superiority. The outcome was clear. It was going to be a perfect slaughter. And what then would happen to Anne?

Holmes turned to Phillips and said, "I'm going to break radio silence and tell the commodore his torpedoes are running too deep."

After a long and thoughtful pause, Phillips said, "He's not going to like that."

"I know," Holmes said. "But somebody has to stick his neck out. Our torpedoes are defective."

He printed the message on an official radio form:

TWELVE TORPEDOES EXPENDED FOR TWO HITS RE-
SULTING IN ONE TRANSPORT SINKING. CAREFUL
ANALYSIS LEADS TO CONCLUSION TORPEDOES RUN-
NING AVERAGE ELEVEN TO FIFTEEN FEET TOO
DEEP. URGENTLY RECOMMEND LIVE FIELD TESTS
ON TARGETS MANILA BAY. SWORDRAY SENDS.

He passed the message to Phillips who scanned it and said, "He's going to accuse you again of undermining faith in our weapons. It could cost you your command, Captain."

"I know it," Holmes said with a deep sigh. He had reached his decision only reluctantly—in what he believed to be the best interest of the U.S. Navy.

The message went off at 1950, just as Fred Bohlen was relieving Henry Slack as officer of the deck. Five minutes later, while Slack was still on the bridge, an aircraft roared out of the darkness at wavetop level.

"Plane! Plane!" a lookout shouted unnecessarily.

"Clear the bridge!" Bohlen cried out in automatic response.

The lookouts, Quartermaster Reed and Slack, jumped down the hatch. Bohlen watched the plane's exhaust fire. It pulled up sharply into the dark sky, rolled, focused a powerful searchlight on *Swordray,* and commenced a run.

"Dive! Dive!" Bohlen shouted into the intercom. At the same time he pulled the bridge diving alarm, then jumped down the hatch, pulling it shut by the lanyard.

"One hundred feet!" he shouted to control. "Sound the collision alarm."

Swordray "hung" momentarily then nosed down at a steep angle. The collision siren whooped throughout the boat.

"That sonofabitch must have homed in on our radio transmission," Bohlen said, eye on the depth gauge.

They heard the splashes as two depth charges fell into the water, one off the starboard bow, one off the port quarter. Both exploded at the same time—beneath *Swordray*. WHAM. WHAM. The boat was caught dead between the two terrifying, deafening explosions. The force blew her upward so violently she broached—came back to the surface. Later, the men would swear that the whole pressure hull twisted a foot or more. Steel deck plates flew up, glass gauges shattered, men were blown off their feet into the bulkheads, some badly cut and bruised.

"Flood negative!" Bohlen shouted when he regained his feet and senses and realized *Swordray* had broached. "Take her *down!*"

"Flooding negative."

Both Holmes and Phillips had been resting in their staterooms when Bohlen dived the boat. Both were putting on their shoes when the depth charges exploded. Both were thrown to the deck, but neither was seriously hurt. They recovered and raced to the conning tower where Bohlen stood, his eyes riveted on the depth gauge which now showed that *Swordray* was going down again.

"A plane came out of nowhere," Bohlen said to Holmes. "They must have a radio direction finder station on Hainan. The charges fell damn close."

"So I heard," Holmes said in his calm way. "Let's hope he doesn't have any more."

"Sixty feet," Les Reed sang out. *Swordray* was going down fast now, reaching for safety.

"Eighty feet."

"Blow negative to the mark," Bohlen ordered. "Zero bubble."

"One hundred feet."

Swordray leveled off. Bohlen turned to the telephone talker, "All compartments report damage."

The damage was slight. A few minor leaks, shattered

dials and gauges, electrical fuses blown. When Bohlen reported this to Holmes, Holmes said, "Lucky for us these boats are built tough."

They remained at one hundred feet, circling at slow speed. No more depth charges fell. After a half-hour, Holmes brought the boat to sixty feet, raised the periscope and carefully searched the sky and water. There was nothing in sight. They surfaced and continued the battery charge and the fruitless patrolling.

The response to Holmes' radio message to Wilkes came at 0340. The watch messenger woke him. Holmes read:

> YOUR MESSAGE RE TORPEDOES BORDERS ON IN-SUBORDINATION. NEITHER YOU NOR ANY OTHER COMMANDING OFFICER SHALL DEVIATE FROM ESTABLISHED BUORD FIRING PROCEDURE. CON-TINUE TO SET DEPTH AS ORDERED. SWORDRAY RETURN TO MANILA FOR FUTHER ASSIGNMENT. ACKNOWLEDGE. WILKES.

It was exactly what he had privately expected. Pig-headed stupidity, blind faith in—or fear of challenging—BuOrd, the sacred cow. Well, he had done his duty as he saw it. If the commodore wanted to relieve him of command, so be it. He got up and scribbled out an acknowl-edgment. Then he woke Phillips to apprise him of the new orders.

Phillips received the news with mixed feelings. There was going to be hell to pay about the torpedoes, he knew, a confrontation with the commodore that could spell professional disaster for the skipper. On the other hand, it could be a chance to see Anne again.

Holmes mind was apparently elsewhere. He said, "Maybe we can find out what happened to Tom Bellinger."

3

Tom Bellinger had passed two of the strangest weeks of his Navy life. He was like a man without a country: no ship, no orders, no I.D. For part of that time, he informally joined the crew of his old ship, the tender *Canopus*, which, camouflaged to look like a pier from the air, was moored at the downtown Manila waterfront. *Canopus* was attempting to provide repair service for the boats returning from brief war patrols. But owing to the incessant and devastating air attacks on Manila, no work could be carried out during daylight. The men of *Canopus* spent most of the day huddling in slit trenches ashore, or manning anti-aircraft batteries, while the subs lay submerged on the bottom of the bay. After dark, the men returned to *Canopus* to work on the boats which surfaced and nested alongside. But most of the technicians were so exhausted they could not work properly.

After the Japanese landings at Lingayen Gulf and Lamon Bay, Wilkes ordered *Canopus* shifted to Corregidor, where she would be under protection of "The Rock's" big guns. Upon learning of this decision, Bellinger decided to leave the ship. It was clear to him that the *Canopus* was going to be sacrificed. Her crew was doomed—like Manila and all of the Philippines. Bellinger had no heart for a last-ditch, anonymous fight to the death—or surrender. Better, he thought, to find a way out of the Philippines, rejoin *Swordray* somewhere, clear his name and give his best in the job he knew best.

So it was that after *Canopus* sailed to Corregidor, Tom Bellinger informally attached himself to the Sixteenth Naval District motor pool, which was bivouacked in a downtown Manila park near the Marsman Building. The pool had only recently—and hastily—been established. It was manned by other sailors like Bellinger who had lost or missed their ships or units and were drifting about homeless.

The various drivers of the motor pool were among the best-informed men in Manila on the progress of the war. They were a mobile outfit; their duties took them all over the city—and beyond. They observed and listened and exchanged information. What it all added up to was pure disaster. MacArthur's new strategy of stopping the Japs on the beaches had utterly failed. The North Defense Force, opposing the Japanese coming from Lingayen Gulf, and the South Defense Force, opposing the Japanese coming from Lamon Bay, were in headlong, desperate retreat. The old strategy—Plan Orange—of falling back to Bataan and Corregidor had, of necessity, been reverted to. The questions were: could the retreating troops reach Bataan before they were cut off, and could they stockpile enough food and medicine on Bataan for a prolonged holding operation? To Bellinger and the other drivers, it seemed highly unlikely.

"Hey, Bellinger!" the old chief who ran the motor pool yelled from his grandly-named "operations tent." "Where the hell's Bellinger?"

"Here!" Bellinger said, getting up. He had been dozing against a tree. He carefully picked his way to the tent in the dark.

"Got a high-priority job," the chief said. "You and Smitty take your trucks over to High Commissioner Sayre's headquarters. They're moving out lock, stock and barrel."

"Where to?" Bellinger asked.

"Corregidor."

"You expect us to drive right across the bay?"

"No, asshole. *You* take their stuff to fleet landing. There'll be a ferry there waiting. Report to a gal named Anne Simpson. She's in charge of the move."

Bellinger and Smitty drove their big trucks to the sandbagged mansion where High Commissioner Sayre and his staff were headquartered. MPs detained them several times to avoid the great masses of troops retreating through the city to Bataan. Along the way, Bellinger kept repeating the name Anne Simpson to himself. He had heard it somewhere before, but he could not remember where.

The vast lawn of the commissioner's mansion was the scene of feverish activity. A Marine work party was carrying out and stacking steel file cabinets. Other Marines were bringing out personal luggage—suitcases, steamer trunks, footlockers. Presiding over the evacuation was a woman holding a clipboard. Bellinger approached her and said, "Anne Simpson?"

"Yes," she said, turning to him with a smile. She looked closely at his insignia and the blue cloth submarine dolphin on his lower right sleeve.

"Bellinger," he said, marveling to himself at the girl's beauty.

Anne Simpson continued staring at the sailor. His name was familiar. She said, "I see you're a submariner. What boat?"

In the two weeks ashore in Manila, not one other person had asked Bellinger that question. Thus he had not revealed his origins and raised further unnecessary or incriminating questions. But he saw no harm in telling this civilian woman the truth.

"Swordray," he answered.

"Swordray!" she exclaimed in mystification. "She's on patrol!"

"Yes, ma'am," Bellinger said. "I missed the sailing." In a way, it was the truth.

"Your executive officer is my . . ." She hesitated a moment, then said, "My fiancé."

"Mister Phillips?" Bellinger said.

"Yes."

"Of course," Bellinger said. "I thought your name was familiar. Is there any news of the boat?"

"Last I heard she was patrolling off Hainan Island," Anne said. "That's top secret."

"Yes," Bellinger said. "I'll keep it to myself." He paused and said, "You're taking *all* those files to Corregidor?"

"I'm afraid so," she said. "No government can exist without files."

"Is the whole government moving to Corregidor?"

"Haven't you heard?" Anne said. "MacArthur just declared Manila an open city. To save it from further destruction. Everybody's moving to Corregidor. Quezon. Sayre. MacArthur. Hart. Wilkes."

"So it's come down to that," Bellinger said.

"I'm afraid so," she answered.

"We better get to work," Bellinger said.

Bellinger and Smitty backed the trucks to the files and luggage. The Marines loaded the trucks while Anne made an inventory on the clipboard. When the loading was finished, she asked Bellinger to sign the inventory with an apology. "No government can operate without red tape."

"Glad to do it," Bellinger said.

"I'll see you at the fleet landing," she said.

On the way, Bellinger considered what he should do now. The motor pool would no doubt be dissolved immediately. His hope of catching a ship out of Manila had evaporated. They were all gone—or sunk. He could flee into the mountains and try to escape to another island somehow. But that seemed like a dangerous long shot. On the spur of the moment, he decided to evacuate himself to Corregidor. Perhaps some submarine calling there, or at *Canopus*, could use an experienced quartermaster.

They backed the trucks up to the ferry moored at fleet landing. Soon Anne Simpson arrived in a staff car to supervise the unloading. A Filipino work party shifted the loads from the trucks to the ferry. During this work, dozens of staff cars and limousines arrived with most of the high brass in the Philippines. The MacArthur party— the general, his wife Jean, their son Arthur and his amah. Admiral Hart and his aides. President Quezon and his family. Sayre and his family. And last, faces familiar to Bellinger, Commodore Wilkes, Captain Fife and Commander Sunshine Murray.

Bellinger was close enough to MacArthur and Quezon to hear an exchange between them.

"Don't worry, Mister President," MacArthur said sonorously, "President Roosevelt has assured me that help is on the way."

"I do not doubt," Quezon replied. "But I wish he would hurry."

"We shall hold," MacArthur said. "Then we'll break out of Bataan and slaughter them."

When the unloading was complete, Anne extended her hand and said to Bellinger, "Well, thanks very much. I don't know what I'd have done without you."

He shook her hand and said, "Glad to help out."

"What will you do now?" she asked.

"I don't know," he said. "Could you use a good quartermaster temporarily? I thought maybe I'd go to the Rock and try to find a billet on a boat. Any boat."

"Sure," she said. "We'd be glad to have a *Swordray* sailor."

When the ferry shoved off, Tom Bellinger stood with Anne Simpson in the bow. On the northern horizon they could see the flashing of heavy field artillery. The Japs would be in Manila within a day. How right Rosaria had been to escape on the *Piet Heyn*.

"Look at the general," Anne said.

MacArthur was standing alone on the small bridge deck above them. He wore a sloppy hat and smoked a big corncob pipe. He was silently staring at the city skyline drawing astern.

"I wonder what's on his mind," Bellinger said.

"Victory," she said.

Chapter Six

1

A PT boat led *Swordray* through the mine field in the mouth of Manila Bay and then into the Corregidor docking area where *Canopus* was moored. *Swordray* nested outboard of Freddie Warder's *Seawolf* and Lou Shane's *Shark*, both returned from war patrol the day before. The Japanese had not yet bombed Corregidor. The technicians on *Canopus* swarmed over *Seawolf* and *Shark* and prepared to take on *Swordray*.

Holmes, wearing starched whites, crossed the brows of *Shark* and *Seawolf* and mounted the gangway of *Canopus*. He learned from the officer of the deck that Commodore Wilkes had set up headquarters in Malinta Tunnel. The O.O.D. arranged a staff car to take Holmes there.

Malinta Tunnel was the largest of the network of tunnels honeycombing Corregidor. It was now jammed with military and civilian evacuees from Manila. MacArthur, Quezon, Sayre, Hart and others had set up operational headquarters in bays off the tunnel. Wilkes, Fife, Murray, a yeoman and a radioman—the Asiatic Fleet Submarine Force staff had been reduced to five men—occupied Bay 14-Z.

Holmes made his way through the busy, noisy tunnel to Bay 14-Z. Wilkes and the yeoman worked at desks fashioned from packing crates. There was one typewriter and a chart of the Far East taped to the cement wall. As Holmes saluted Wilkes he was thinking, here is a man who has worn himself out. Wilkes perfunctorily invited Holmes to sit—on a spare-parts box.

Without ceremony, Wilkes said, "Holmes, you deliberately violated two explicit orders. You set your torpedoes to run shallow; you broke radio silence and almost lost your boat as a consequence. Moreover, you've done the Navy a grave disservice by again undermining faith in our torpedoes. *There is nothing wrong with the Mark Fourteen torpedo!*"

"But, sir," Holmes said, "we shot twelve . . ."

"It's your fire control party," Wilkes said. "They obviously don't know their jobs. And that's *your* fault, Holmes. You went out there and wasted twelve precious torpedoes. In light of the shortage of torpedoes, that's almost criminal."

"Sir, those torpedoes are running too deep," Holmes insisted. "Too deep for the magnetic exploder to work. To send us to sea with those torpedoes, *that's* criminal."

Wilkes stared at Holmes with rage in his eyes. "If you criticize our torpedoes one more time—to me or anyone else—I'll have you court-martialed."

"Sir," Holmes pressed. "Would you authorize me to conduct a live test? I'll string a fish net underwater and fire. . . ."

"No!" Wilkes shouted. "There's no *time* for a test. We're pulling out of here tomorrow morning for Java. *Shark* will take Admiral Hart and his staff. You will take me and my staff and some others I pick."

"To Java?"

"Yes. Surabaya. When we reach Surabaya, you will be relieved of command."

Holmes thought he was inwardly steeled for the sentence. He had known it was inevitable. But when it was pronounced, he was shocked. Relief from command in combat for cause was a professional disaster. There would be no recovery from it. Even though his father-in-law had been a much-respected rear admiral, Holmes would never earn four stripes now. The old-boy network could only help so much. It could not override this. After the war, he'd retire at his present rank—commander.

But he was careful to give no outward sign of his shock. "I'll need fuel oil," he said evenly.

"There *is* no goddamned fuel oil," Wilkes raved. "That asshole MacArthur ordered all the fuel oil in Manila destroyed, without checking with Hart or anybody else. Can you top that for stupidity? That's why we have to leave. Ask Lou Shane if he can give you ten thousand gallons. He filled up before the oil was destroyed."

"Aye, aye," Holmes said, rising.

"I'll send you a list of your passengers by 1800," Wilkes said.

Holmes saluted, started to leave, then asked, "Sir, by any chance, do you know what happened to my quartermaster Tom Bellinger?"

"Who?"

"Quartermaster Tom Bellinger," Holmes said. "The man O.N.I. had charged with espionage. He was in the Cavite brig when they bombed the base."

"I've heard nothing," Wilkes said, returning to his paperwork.

Holmes eased out of the bay into the main tunnel. He returned to *Canopus,* descended the brow to *Shark.* He found Lou Shane in the wardroom talking to Freddie Warder, who was so highly agitated he failed even to notice that Holmes was present.

"When we got to Aparri, there was a tin can guarding the mouth of the harbor," Warder was saying to Shane. "We eased by him and went into the harbor. There was a big seaplane tender at anchor. An absolute dead duck. We set up at 3800 yards and fired four bow tubes, two set to run at forty feet, two for thirty feet. Absolutely nothing happened. No explosions. No flame. No smoke. We turned to run out and fired the four stern tubes from 4500 yards. Again, not a single explosion! Eight fish shot at an *anchored* target. No hits! Boy, did the commodore chew *me* out. But I tell you, Lou, there's something drastically wrong with these torpedoes!" He fell silent.

"We got two hits out of twelve shots," Holmes said quietly.

Warder turned to see who had spoken. "Oh, hello, Hunt. How goes it?" They shook hands, then Holmes shook hands with Shane.

"The commodore has given me absolute orders not to criticize the torpedoes," Holmes said. "And I won't. But let me say this. The two that hit were set to run at ten feet."

"Yeah?" Warder said. "Ten feet, eh? So it was you who provoked that rocket from Wilkes?"

"None other." He sat down. "And royally chewed out for it. How about you, Lou?" The steward served him coffee.

"We didn't see a single target," Shane said. "I wish we'd been at Lingayen Gulf."

"Hear what happened to Mort Mumma?" Warder said. "Got jumped by a tin can and cracked up. Asked to be locked in his cabin. The exec brought the boat back to Manila."

Holmes sipped his coffee, deeply disturbed. Mort Mumma, skipper of *Sailfish*, had won all the peacetime awards. He was considered the squadron standout. "Isn't that terrible?" he said aloud, "I wonder what happened?"

"His torpedoes missed," Warder said bitterly. "Or failed to explode. If they'd hit, if he'd gotten that tin can, he'd be a hero instead of a bum. What the hell are we going to do?"

"Set them to run shallow and fudge the logbooks?" Shane ventured.

"That's no way to fight a goddamned war," Warder said.

"You can't go over his head," Holmes said. "He'll relieve you. He's scared to death of challenging BuOrd."

"He's in the selection zone," Warder said. "Bucking for two stars. The way he planned the defense of Lingayen Gulf, I'd say he better forget those two stars. He'll be lucky if he keeps his four stripes."

"Lou," Holmes said, anxious to change the subject and get on to his urgent problem, "the commodore told me to get ten thousand gallons of fuel from you. Can you spare it?"

"Sure," Shane said. "Going to Java, too?"

"Yes," Holmes said. "We're taking the commodore and what's left of his staff and some others. Well, thanks for the fuel. I'll send over my fuel king to make the arrangements."

He left the two skippers discussing the torpedo problem. Warder was right. A way had to be found to get the

problem out in the open. It was near treasonous to pretend
it didn't exist.

2

When Phillips had finished going over the list of needed
repairs with the *Canopus* refit officer-in-charge, he left
Swordray and went immediately to Malinta Tunnel. He
found the High Commissioner's headquarters established in
Bay 20-A. It was jammed with file cabinets. Anne Simpson
was sitting at a desk typing. He walked up behind her and
kissed her on the top of the head. She spun around, gasped
with astonishment and delight. Then she jumped up and
fell into his arms.

"Thank God you're safe," he whispered, kissing her
again and again.

"And you," she said.

"Let's find some privacy," he said.

She laughed lightly and said, "You must be kidding.
There are ten thousand people on this rock. Every square
inch is occupied."

"Where do you live?"

"In the nurses' dorm," she said. "Down the tunnel.
No men allowed."

"Outside then?"

"All right."

They made their way out of the tunnel and found a
vacant patch of grass beneath a huge banyan tree. They sat
down, close together.

"The Japs are in Manila," she said.

"Yes, I know," he said. "You're in grave danger here,
Anne. You've got to get out."

"Danger?" she said, surprised. "Corregidor is impregnable. We can hold out until help comes."

"What help?"

"The President has promised MacArthur the Philippines will not be lost. He's sending ammo, planes, food."

"How is it going to get here?"

"The fleet will bring it."

"Anne!" he said in exasperation. "There *is* no fleet.

Haven't they told you that? The fleet was lost at Pearl Harbor. There's no way anything other than a submarine can get through to Corregidor. And they can't bring in enough to make a particle of difference."

"But why would the President publicly make that promise?" she said. "Why haven't MacArthur and Quezon evacuated—or at least evacuated their families?"

"He made that promise either out of total ignorance of the true situation, or to keep up your morale or for some other reason. The reality is the promise cannot be kept. The Jap Navy is good—far better than any of us believed. They've blockaded the Philippines and there's no way to break it. You'll be stuck here until you run out of food or surrender."

"MacArthur is preparing a counter-attack," she insisted. "He's going to break out of Bataan."

"That's impossible," he said. "Those Filipino draftees can't fight. Not Homma's regulars. It would be another slaughter. Anne, MacArthur is dealing in pipe dreams. His pride prevents him from conceding defeat. He is beaten and beaten good, and you have to get out of here."

"Why can't you submariners smash the blockade?" she asked. "Sink their ships."

"To be perfectly honest, we don't know what we're doing. The Hart-Wilkes submarine defense of the Philippines was the dumbest operation in the history of naval warfare. Wilkes simply has no idea what it's all about." He paused, then went on. "There's another problem. There is something wrong with our torpedoes. One torpedo should sink a ship. We shot twelve and got one lousy troop transport. Other skippers risked their boats and got nothing. Everybody's lost confidence in the weapon. And Wilkes refuses to do anything about it—or even concede there's a problem."

They fell silent, picking at the blades of grass. After a time, she said, "By the way, your quartermaster, Tom Bellinger, is here. He's working for us."

"Really?" he said, astonished. "Thank God for that. But how the hell did he wind up with you?"

She explained. Then she said, "The other night he told me the whole story."

"He was being railroaded," Phillips said.

"It seems that way," she said. "But I don't see any need for worry anymore. The O.N.I. man who was handling the case—Lieutenant Weller?—was killed at Cavite. Tom found his briefcase and burned the files. I'd think that if you took Bellinger aboard *Swordray* and got him out of here, that would be the end of it."

"You're sure about Weller and the files?" he said excitedly.

"That's what he told me."

"Good," he said. "Where is he now?"

"He took some papers up to MacArthur's living quarters—Topside. He should be back soon." She paused. "What's next for *Swordray*? When do you go on patrol again?"

"Tomorrow," he said. "The Navy is pulling out, Anne. Everybody. We're falling back to Java."

This news made her very angry. "Why is the Navy deserting?"

"For one thing, there's no more fuel oil here. MacArthur had the oil stocks destroyed when he abandoned Manila. He apparently didn't check with Hart first."

They fell silent again. Then he went on. "I think the Navy has a more realistic view of the situation than the Army. That's why I insist you get out of here. All of you civilians should leave, from Sayre on down."

"Sayre can't leave if MacArthur stays," she said. "How would that look?"

"Dammit, Anne," he exploded. "You're worrying about appearances; I'm worrying about your *life*."

An air-raid siren mounted on a nearby telephone pole began to moan. They jumped up and ran for the tunnel, holding hands. A minute or so later, the tunnel shook and echoed with the reports of the anti-aircraft guns. Then the bombs began to fall. The whole island seemed to shudder under the impact.

"God!" Phillips said. "Must be five-hundred pounders."

Anne was frightened. She snuggled close against him, arms around his waist.

"This is just the beginning," he said. "They won't stop

until ... until Corregidor capitulates. Will you get it through your thick skull? Corregidor is a *Titanic*."

3

After the all-clear, Phillips hurried back to *Canopus* and *Swordray*. The ships had been spared. Most of the bombs had fallen on the Army barracks area Topside. He found Holmes in the wardroom, writing a letter home. Holmes looked up and said, "Did you find her?"

"Yes," Phillips said. "She's okay, so far. I found Tom Bellinger, too." He explained briefly what had happened to Bellinger, to Weller and the file.

"Well, thank God for small favors," Holmes commented. "Of course, we'll take him aboard. And just forget the whole thing."

"I thought as much," Phillips said. "I've sent Reed to fetch him."

"Good," Holmes said. "By the way, there's something I didn't tell you that you should know. When we reach Java, I'll be relieved of command. He'd do it now, but he hasn't got a spare skipper."

Phillips turned ashen-faced. "That sonofabitch!"

"George, take it easy. He *is* the force commander."

"He's an absolute asshole!"

"He did exactly as you predicted."

"And that makes him an asshole," Phillips said bitterly. "Captain, this is an outrage. You're the best skipper in this outfit. I'm going straight to Hart."

"You'll do no such thing," Holmes said sternly. "This is still the U.S. Navy. And *you* will stay in line. That's an order, Mister Phillips."

Phillips seethed. "If anybody should be relieved of command, it's that ass ... it's the Commodore."

"How is Anne?" Holmes said, deliberately changing the subject.

"Fine," Phillips said, calming down. "But they're not evacuating. It's madness. MacArthur has convinced everybody they can hold out."

"Until?"

"Until the so-called help comes," Phillips said. "It's like Alice in Wonderland."

Holmes considered this for a time and then said, "They should at least be evacuating the women and children."

"At least," Phillips echoed. "But as far as Anne knows, there's not even a contingency plan for that."

There was a sharp rap on the passageway bulkhead. "Come in," Holmes said.

Tom Bellinger walked in beaming. "Afternoon, Captain. Mister Phillips. Quartermaster Bellinger reporting aboard, sir."

"Am I glad to see *you!*" Holmes said heartily. "Have a seat."

Bellinger sat down. At Holmes' request, he recounted his experiences. Holmes had but one question. "You're sure it was the whole file?"

"It looked like it, sir."

"Then the matter is done with," Holmes said. He turned to Phillips. "Destroy all the paperwork on the boat relating to this incident."

"Thanks, Captain," Bellinger said with deep feeling. "I'll never forget this."

"Don't thank me," Holmes said. "You got yourself out of it. I let you down. Anyway, I'm glad it worked out. And we're damned glad to have our quartermaster back."

"That's for sure," Phillips said. "Speaking of which, we sail for Java tomorrow. You better see if *Canopus* has the charts we'll need."

"Aye, aye," Bellinger said, rising to leave. "Why Java?"

"The whole outfit's pulling out," Holmes said. "No more fuel oil. They've got oil in Java. And the Japs haven't landed there."

"The Army won't like this," Bellinger said.

"Can't be helped," Holmes said. "*They* destroyed the oil stocks."

Bellinger said to Phillips, "After I finish the charts, may I have permission to go to the tunnel? I left some things there. And I'd like to say goodbye to some people."

"Certainly," Phillips said. "And while you're there,

will you please tell Anne Simpson that our dinner will be delayed until 1800 tonight? She's coming aboard to eat with us."

"If I may say so, sir," Bellinger said, "she's a real fine lady. And *brainy*. My God, she's sharp! She runs that whole headquarters. You're a very lucky man. I hope she . . ." he broke off the thought.

"Thanks, Tom," Phillips said. "I hope so, too."

4

After dinner, Phillips escorted Anne Simpson back to the tunnel in pitch darkness. They were stopped every ten feet, it seemed, by security patrols and roadblocks. A security guard blocked their way at the tunnel entrance. A curfew had been imposed. No unauthorized personnel were to be admitted to the tunnel after curfew. The orders were absolute.

"So, it's goodbye here," Phillips said, leading her over to a sandbagged anti-aircraft emplacement. "Like dropping a girl off at her front door. Some front door."

They were silent, holding hands. Then he said, "I feel terrible going off and leaving you in danger like this, Anne. If there was *any* way at all I could stay, I would."

"Please don't feel badly, George," she said, combing his hair with her fingers. "I'll be all right. You have a job to do and I have a job to do. That's all there is to it."

"This damned war," he said bitterly.

"We have the future," she said. "Tomorrow is another day."

They fell silent again, both hating the moment. She sought a way to take his mind from it. "By the way, thanks for dinner. That was the best meal I've had in a long, long time."

He said firmly, "Anne, no help is coming. You've got to get out of here."

She put her finger on his lips. "We agreed we wouldn't discuss that anymore."

He nodded, kissing her finger. Then he said, "Damn. Damn. Damn. Damn."

She said, "George, there is something I want to tell you."

"Yes?"

"I love you very much, George. I always will. This ... the war ... when it's over, we'll find one another again. Somewhere. Then, yes, if you still want me, I'll marry you."

She looked at him with loving eyes. He held her close and kissed her. After a time, she said, "Please go now. I can't take this anymore. It is pure torture."

"Yes," he said. "It is torture."

She kissed him one last time and said, "Fair breeze, sailor. God watch over you."

"And you."

She ran for the tunnel, sobbing. He turned away, tears streaming down his cheek.

Chapter Seven

1

Commodore Wilkes, Captain Fife and Commander Murray came aboard *Swordray* at 0800. The yeoman and radioman followed behind carrying the typewriter, the War Diary and a few other classified papers. An hour later, a truck brought twenty-five other passengers. These were Navy personnel—mostly submarine technicians—whom Wilkes had ordered to evacuate Corregidor. They were not unhappy about leaving.

Another of the spunky little PT boats led *Swordray* through the mine field to open water. On the bridge, Tom Bellinger took a final look at *Canopus*. A valiant ship, he thought, a great crew. As he had long ago surmised, Wilkes and Hart had decreed that she would be left behind. She was too old and slow to make a run for it. If she tried, they had said, she would surely be caught at sea by Jap bombers and sunk with the loss of all hands. Although he'd known it was inevitable, Bellinger did not agree with that decision. They had discounted the ship's famous luck.

Belowdecks, *Swordray* resembled a teeming ant hill. She carried a total of thirty extra passengers. They had spread out along the passageways, or doubled up in unoccupied nooks and crannies, wherever they could find space to sit down. Those going fore and aft through the ten compartments had to thread their way carefully. The strain on the two mess galley cooks was evident. There were now six meal seatings three times a day, instead of

102

the customary two, compelling the cooks to work eighteen hours a day straight through. The addition of Wilkes, Fife, Murray and four other officers had likewise imposed a heavy strain on the wardroom mess steward Leroy Collins.

No group felt the load more heavily than *Swordray*'s radiomen. *Swordray* was now COMSUBASIATIC headquarters. From her wardroom, Wilkes, Fife and Murray were attempting to run the other twenty-seven submarines —seventeen on war patrol, ten en route to Java with hand-picked Corregidor evacuees. The radio traffic to and from *Swordray* was immense, forcing the radiomen to stand continuous watches, getting by on catnaps.

The boat's crew stood regular watches. As if on war patrol, they were tense, alert. *Swordray* was in enemy-controlled waters. Nobody had any clear idea at that time where the "front lines" lay. Japanese task forces were reported daily, all over the charts. At any moment, one— or a land-based aircraft—might barrel over the horizon and catch *Swordray* on the surface in broad daylight.

The wardroom had been divided into two meal seatings. Wilkes, Fife, Murray, Holmes and Phillips took the first seating. The ship's junior officers—Slack, Bohlen and Nolan—sat with the four officer-passengers in the second.

The first noon meal that day was a distinctly awkward and uneasy time for Holmes and Phillips. Holmes, the condemned man, had to break bread face to face with his executioners. Murray, as usual, tried to alleviate the situation with cheery banter, but Wilkes and Fife were preoccupied with a grave new problem. Too many skippers had failed to perform "aggressively" on their first brief patrols. They had not gone in harm's way. They had evaded and fudged, hesitating to engage the enemy. Holmes and Phillips were shocked speechless to learn that in addition to Mort Mumma, Wilkes had relieved four other skippers in Manila. That was one reason there was a shortage of skippers; and why Holmes' own relief had been postponed to Java.

"A man looks outstanding in peacetime," Wilkes said to Fife, talking as though Holmes and Phillips were not present, "then he falls on his face under fire. I don't understand it, Jimmy. Then, take the opposite case. Take that Gene McKinney. A lawyer, for God's sake, and the shyest man I ever met. A regular Caspar Milquetoast. Yet he takes *Salmon* up to Lingayen Gulf and is fearless as they come. How do you explain it?"

"The British had the same problem early in the war," Fife said. It was the first time either Holmes or Phillips had ever heard Fife speak. His voice was high-pitched, tinny. "The Royal Navy made a comprehensive study. Some thought athletes made the most aggressive skippers. Others thought the intellectuals. Still others thought the misfits and troublemakers. They could never reach any valid conclusions. Too much human nature—human motivation—involved. You simple cannot forecast, or quantify, courage."

"How did they deal with it operationally?" Wilkes asked.

"Simple," Fife answered. "They gave every qualified skipper two war patrols to show his stuff. If he didn't sink any ships in two patrols, out he went."

"A tough policy," Holmes put in. "Sometimes luck plays a big role in sightings and sinkings."

"Have to be tough," Fife said sternly. "No room in submarine warfare for overcaution."

"Captain to the bridge!" the wardroom intercom shattered the talk. It was the duty O.O.D., Bill Nolan.

Holmes grabbed his hat and raced topside to the bridge, Phillips right behind him.

"Smoke on the horizon dead ahead," Nolan explained excitedly.

Holmes examined the distant smoke puffs with his binoculars. Directly below, in the conning tower, Tom Bellinger raised number two periscope to its fullest height and put his eye into the eyepiece, focusing dead ahead. His "eyes" were now far above the men on the bridge and thus he could see much farther over the curvature of the earth. What he saw brought his heart to his mouth: the upper tips of heavy tripod top-hampers.

He punched the intercom switch. "Captain, Bellinger on high periscope. Looks like a task force. Battlewagons or heavy cruisers." He gave details.

"Very well, Tom," Holmes said. "Station the tracking party. . . . No. Belay that last word. Go to battle stations."

"Battle stations, aye."

Bellinger rang the alarm. By then, word of the contact had spread through the boat and the crew was already picking its way through the passageway to battle stations. Within one minute, all hands were ready. In the jammed conning tower, Phillips presided over the approach party —the TDC and the small hand-plot group that backed up the TDC. Bellinger served as Phillips' general assistant.

Wilkes and Fife made their way up the ladder to the bridge. "What's all this about?" Wilkes asked Holmes.

"Task force, Commodore," Holmes said in his calm way. "Headed directly this way."

The smoke puffs were gone but from the bridge they could now just make out the low forest of maststicks through binoculars. There had been no change in course. The force was coming on relentlessly.

"I plan to dive in five minutes, Commodore," Holmes said. "I'll pick a battleship for the primary target. Fire all six tubes forward. Then set up on the next best available target with the stern tubes."

Wilkes stared at him as though he were mad. Then he said icily, "You'd actually make an attack with the Force Commander, his staff and twenty-five passengers aboard?"

Holmes was stunned. He did not know what to say.

"Those ships will be escorted by a dozen tin cans," Wilkes went on. "If you attack, *Swordray* will be lost. What would then happen to the other twenty-seven boats? They'd have no command, no orders. It would be chaos."

Holmes looked evenly at Wilkes, not believing his ears. Only ten minutes ago, Wilkes and Fife had been pontificating about courage, and lack of it. An attack on an enemy task force would be risky, but not necessarily fatal to *Swordray*. There was a good chance—perhaps even odds—they could get away with it. Wilkes knew that. Where were his courage and aggressiveness?

"Those are very valuable enemy ships," Holmes said. "I feel it is my duty to attack them."

"Your duty is to deliver us to Java, Holmes," Wilkes said. "Break off the attack and evade at best speed."

"But, sir . . ."

"Break off the attack!" Wilkes said. "That's an order."

Holmes conceded. He could see there was no point in further debate. He punched the intercom. "Right full rudder. All ahead flank. Secure from battle stations. The commodore has ordered us to break off the attack in the best interests of our passengers."

2

The harbor at Surabaya, Java, was jammed with shipping of every description: American, British, Australian men-of-war; merchant ships of every nationality. As required and customary, *Swordray* took aboard a native pilot and stood up the channel until they found *Holland* moored at a Dutch Navy pier. They maneuvered alongside and nested on her outboard, or port, side, a very welcome breast indeed.

Wilkes, Fife and Murray departed *Swordray* as soon as the brow was over. Wilkes had no departing words for Holmes, not even the customary thank you called for in Navy ettiquette. Phillips, however, observing the departure from the brow, had a few words for the Commodore. They were muttered too low, he thought, for Wilkes to hear: "So long, you sonofabitch."

But Holmes had heard. "What did I tell you, Mister Phillips? If you do that again, I'm going to put you in hack."

There was much work to be done to *Swordray*. The technicians on *Canopus* had performed well, but *Holland* was her "home" tender, and now many larger jobs that had been deferred were ordered: engine and hydraulic pump overhaul; new electric hoist motor for Number Two periscope; installation of a new sound head; repainting, and so on. In addition, at Holmes' special request, *Swordray*'s bridge silhouette was reduced considerably by cutting away parts of the steel "sail" that enclosed the bridge from the weather. His bridge would be wetter, but far more difficult for the enemy to see.

Holmes and Phillips went about these tasks, grateful for old and willing friends in the *Holland*'s repair gang, but all the while with a feeling of foreboding. They were waiting for the other shoe to drop, the new skipper to report on board. But, again, the relief had been deferred. On arrival in Surabaya, Wilkes had gone immediately to confer with Hart, who had established a combined allied naval headquarters in the mountains of Java near Lembang. Wilkes was away for a full week.

Meanwhile, as they learned from Tokyo Rose and a few official messages, the Japanese were moving ever southward toward Java. Borneo, the Celebes, New Guinea and the Solomon Islands fell quickly. (When Rabaul capitulated, Tom Bellinger remembered Juanita and her copra-planter husband and wondered how they had fared.) In the Philippines, only Bataan and Corregidor still held out, and in Malaysia, only Singapore. But rumors abounded that MacArthur was running out of food and ammo; that the British and Australians in Malaysia were being badly routed by bicycle-riding Japanese shock troops.

When Wilkes returned to *Holland*, he immediately summoned Holmes to his shipboard office. Wilkes still looked and acted like a man at the end of his rope—hollow-eyed and haggard.

"Holmes," he said, "you've been granted a reprieve. We're still short of skippers who're looking for a fight. I want you to take *Swordray* on a special mission."

In a way, Holmes felt disappointment. He would rather have it done, get it over with. Get out, get on to something else where he could work for people he could respect. He might even be lucky enough to draw an assignment in BuOrd headquarters. If so, he might influence them to live-test the Mark Fourteen torpedo. So far as he had been able to learn, Wilkes had not made one complaint to BuOrd about the torpedoes.

Wilkes went on. "I want you to unload all ballast and all but six torpedoes in your forward tubes and take a maximum load of food and ammo to Corregidor."

"What?" Holmes said, again scarcely able to believe the words coming from Wilkes' mouth.

"You heard me right the first time," Wilkes said. He held up his hand. "I know, don't say it. You're a combatant ship, not a grocery and supply barge. You should be sinking enemy men-of-war. In any event, you can only carry a drop in the bucket, et cetera, et cetera. I know all that. Admiral Hart knows all that. He protested to Washington. But the orders came down from the White House itself. The President wants a dramatic gesture made to help those poor bastards on Bataan and Corregidor. For the sake of their morale. Only a sub can reach Corregidor now. And you are going to do it."

"Aye, aye, sir," Holmes said. Protesting further was clearly useless.

"And remember," Wilkes went on. "Those six torpedoes are purely *defensive* armament. You're not to seek out and attack the enemy. Use your torpedoes *only* if you are attacked. Is that clear?"

"Yes, sir," Holmes said.

"And if you have to use them, go strictly by the book," Wilkes said. "No tampering with depth settings."

"Yes, sir," Holmes repeated. But he was lying. If he had to use torpedoes, he would set them to run at ten feet, not thirty or forty, and damn the consequences.

"One more thing," Wilkes said.

"Sir?"

"Maintain absolute radio silence," Wilkes said. "No more cry-baby messages about the torpedoes. Is that clear?"

"Yes, sir, Commodore."

Sunshine Murray had prepared the operation order. When he turned it over to Holmes in his office, he said, "I know this is tough, Hunt. You don't deserve what you're getting. For God's sake, don't quote me, but I'm beginning to suspect you may be right about the torpedoes. You're not the only skipper to raise a beef. But Hunt, try to understand the Commodore's position. If he conceded the torpedoes were defective . . ." He paused and sighed. "Put it this way. They're all we have to fight with."

"Sunshine," Holmes said earnestly, "all I've ever asked for is a live test. If they're running deep, they can be fixed with a simple adjustment to the rudder throws."

"He feels that if he conducts a test, he'll further undermine the faith," Murray said.

"That's absurd," Holmes said. "There *is* no faith."

"I've gone to bat for you, Hunt," Murray said sadly.

"A dozen times. But I lost every time. I'm afraid if I try again I'll be sacked too."

"Well I appreciate that very much, Sunshine," Holmes said.

"Don't worry about it," Murray said. "It's going to be a long war. You can't keep a good man down, as they say. You'll pop back."

But they both knew that was not so.

He shook hands and said, "Thanks again, Sunshine. Good luck."

"Good luck to you and *Swordray*," Murray said, adding with a grin, "I'd have gone for that Jap task force, too."

When Phillips heard all this news, he was again emotionally torn. He was unspeakably happy—and relieved—that Holmes was to retain command of *Swordray* for another patrol. He hoped that in the meantime, by some miracle, something—not minor—would happen to Wilkes or that the proposed relief would be forgotten. But he was furious that *Swordray* was to be withdrawn from combat and converted to a supply barge and thought that their assigned mission to Corregidor for "morale purposes" was absurdly dangerous. On the other hand, he was deliriously happy at the prospect of seeing Anne again. This trip he *had* to help her. And he had an idea toward that end. The plan began to take shape deep in the recesses of his mind.

In the next twenty-four hours, *Swordray*'s crew, assisted by *Holland* work parties, toiled as it never had. Twenty tons of lead ballast were removed from the lower bilges. All the torpedoes save six in the forward tubes were also transferred to *Holland*. On board *Swordray* came six hundred and sixty cases of fifty-caliber machine-gun ammo—one million rounds—and six tons of rice in two hundred pound bags. Every inch of space inside the submarine was utilized for storing these supplies.

When all this work had been completed and the extra weight compensated for in the main ballast and trim systems, they topped off the fuel tanks from *Holland* and once more set off for the bastion of Corregidor.

Standing down the channel, *Swordray* passed an in-

coming ship. They saw from her lines that she was an
ancient Dutch passenger liner. She had been badly bombed
and strafed and had a hard port list.

As she drew aft, Tom Bellinger, out of long-standing
habit, turned to check the name on the stern. To his
amazement, he saw it was the *Piet Heyn*. He quickly
grabbed the signal light and flashed it at her fast-receding
bridge. He received an instant "go ahead" from the sig-
nalman on *Piet Heyn*.

WHERE FROM? Bellinger signalled.
SINGAPORE, came the reply.
HOW GOES SINGAPORE?
BAD. CAN'T LAST LONG. NO AIR POWER.
WE HIT ON WAY OUT.
YOU HAVE PASSENGERS?
YES. FULL TO CAPACITY.
GOOD LUCK.
GOOD HUNTING, *Piet Heyn* returned.

Shutting off the light, Bellinger wondered about Rosaria. Jolly, fat, rich Rosaria. Singapore would hold, she
had said. The British would fight. Had she got off in
Singapore or had she stayed on *Piet Heyn?* Had she been
at the rail wondering what boat they might be? Wondering
where her fortune might be? What would she think if she
knew it was going back to Corregidor in the Captain's
safe?

3

A PT boat led *Swordray* through the mine fields into
Corregidor after dark, to avoid Japanese bombers which
were pounding the Rock daily. She moored at the pier
where *Canopus* was berthed. The tender had been hit
several times and appeared to be a wreck. Her topside was
mauled, smoke poured from somewhere in the bow, she
listed heavily to starboard. In fact, they learned, belowdecks *Canopus* was still a humming repair factory, sup-

porting the ground forces on Corregidor. The topside damage was real, but the smoke came from a smudge-pot and the list had been deliberately put on to give the impression she was an abandoned hulk not worth another bomb.

Her skipper, Earl Sackett, was standing on the pier when *Swordray*'s brow went over. He came aboard, saluting smartly.

"Welcome to Corregidor," he said to Holmes, who met him on the forward deck.

"How are things?" Holmes said, returning the salute.

"The bombers have been giving us fits," Sackett said. "MacArthur's forces on Bataan have just completed a withdrawal to the Bagac-Orion line. That's about halfway down the peninsula. Homma is pushing hard. Our boys are critically short of food, medicine and ammo. They're eating monkeys in the jungle. Other than that, everything is fine. Now, sir, how can *Canopus* help you?"

Holmes was deeply moved. In spite of all, *Canopus* was still holding out, offering services. He said, "We just need a few voyage repairs. Nothing big. We've brought food and ammo. We'll need some help with the unloading if you can spare some working parties."

"Food and ammo!" Sackett exclaimed. "That's marvelous."

"Not much," Holmes said, giving the details.

Sackett then took a Top Secret radio dispatch from his pocket and said, "Did you get this CNO dispatch about the radio communications group?"

"No," said Holmes.

"CNO wants you to evacuate the whole group and their gear."

"How many are there?"

"Fifty-one."

"Fifty-one!" Holmes exclaimed. "I'm not sure we can take that many."

"Then you'll have to off-load some of your crew to make room," Sackett said. "The evacuees have highest priority."

"I'll *make* room. There's no way I'm going to leave

any of my crew in this place. Who the hell are these people, anyway? Why should they be evacuated before anybody else?"

"I'm not sure who they are," Sackett said. "All I know is that CNO insists they be taken out as soon as possible."

"Well, I guess I have no choice. Are they ready to go? I want to get out of here before dawn."

"All packed and waiting," Sackett said.

"Good," Holmes said. "By the way, I have orders from Commodore Wilkes to draw eighteen torpedoes from you and all the spare parts we can cram aboard. My engineering officer has a list of what's needed."

Sackett nodded. "Okay, we better get started."

Henry Slack walked up and saluted. Holmes introduced the men, adding, "Slack will oversee our unloading and loading."

George Phillips joined the group. After the introductions, he said to Holmes, "I won't be long, Captain. Two hours at the most."

"Where are you headed?" Sackett asked.

"Malinta Tunnel."

"I'll arrange a staff car for you," Sackett said. "You don't want to be walking around in the dark. The dogfaces out there are trigger-happy."

On the way to the tunnel, the driver, a young seaman, said to Phillips, "You got a billet open on that boat for a seaman first?"

"Afraid not, sailor."

"I'm a good worker."

"Sorry."

The driver was silent a moment, then he said bitterly, "That bastard, Dugout Doug. He led us down the garden path, all right."

"Dugout Doug?"

"MacArthur," the sailor said, almost spitting. "Haven't you heard the song?"

"No."

"Dugout Doug MacArthur lies ashaking on the Rock/Safe from all the bombers and from any sudden shock/Dugout Doug is eating of the best food on Bataan/And his troops go starving on."

"Mmmmm," Phillips said.

"He's been over to Bataan *once* since we got here," the sailor said, even more bitterly. "He took food from the troops on Bataan so they could eat better on the Rock. Now the boys on Bataan are starving, and that's a fact."

The car stopped at the heavily sandbagged mouth of the tunnel. Phillips asked the driver to wait, then went inside the tunnel, where he was stopped by security guards. The head guard telephoned the nurses' dorm. After a considerable wait, Anne was on the phone.

"George!" she shrieked in astonishment. "What are you doing here? What . . . ? Never mind. I'll dress and be there in a minute."

She was as good as her word. She ran up, wearing a lime linen dress. She looked beautiful. They embraced and kissed fervently, then left the tunnel and sat on the bluff under the banyan tree, arms around each other.

"Anne," he said. "There's not much time. We're leaving in an hour. Go pack your things. I have permission from the Captain to take you out on *Swordray*."

She was silent for a very long time. He said impatiently, "Hurry up, Anne. We've got to go soon."

She looked at him. "I can't go, George."

"Anne! You've got to go!"

"No," she said sadly. "I can't. Mrs. MacArthur and Mrs. Sayre and the children are still here. And all the nurses. I can't just slip off and desert them."

"Please, Anne. The Japs are halfway down the Bataan Peninsula. There's not much time left."

"Help is on the way."

"No it isn't. We brought some food and ammunition, but it's only a drop in the bucket. Even if we put every sub we had into Corregidor re-supply, we still couldn't bring enough to do any good. And no other ship can get through."

"There's a food convoy en route from Australia."

"Who told you that?"

"We heard it on the radio."

"It's not true. It's propaganda. The Japs are ready to strike Java, the Malaya barrier. No convoy could get through. Anne, believe me, it's all over for MacArthur. His rhetoric can't stop Jap bullets."

She was silent again. "Please, Anne," he begged.

"I'd be a deserter."

"You're not a soldier," he said earnestly. "Anne, be sensible. What good can you do here? If you got out, you could go back home and fight on. Do something worthwhile. Why go down with the *Titanic?* Get in the lifeboat."

She did not reply.

"Go get your things," he said sternly.

"No," she said. "George, I can't explain it, but please try to understand. I can't slip off and save myself and leave all those other women and children here. If they could leave, too, I would go. But I'd never have any peace again if I ran out on them now. My duty is here. You're a sailor. You understand the meaning of duty."

He nodded. He was shaken. He knew she was dedicated and stubborn, but he had expected she would give in this time. Obviously she was not going to give in, and he was horribly afraid she was going to die on Corregidor.

She stood up and extended her hand. "Thank you, George. And thank Hunter for me. That was very decent of him. I'll never forget it. And please say goodbye to Tom for me."

"What is this handshake business?" he demanded, pulling her into his arms.

"I'm trying to be strong," she whispered.

4

Tom Bellinger was assigned to the loading detail as an assistant to Slack in keeping track of every article going aboard and its weight. He logged in the full name, rank and serial number of all fifty-one members of the Navy communications group. He reported to Slack, "Fifty-one men at an average weight of one-eighty is nine thousand one hundred and eighty pounds. They said the gear in those boxes weighs about three thousand pounds. Total: twelve thousand, one-eighty. Six tons."

"Okay," Slack said, noting this on his poop sheet. They had already logged the weight of the spare parts and torpedoes from *Canopus*. After some calculating, Slack said to Bellinger, "We're still going to need a lot of ballast."

A staff car pulled on the pier. George Phillips got out and thanked the driver. He walked up, long-faced.

"Where's Anne?" Slack asked.

Phillips sighed deeply. "She wouldn't come."

Neither Slack nor Bellinger said anything. Phillips broke the silence. "She feels its her duty to stay."

"I'm sorry, George. That's very tough."

"How is she?" Bellinger said.

"Good," Phillips said. "She said to tell you good-bye."

"George," Slack said, changing the subject, "we're going to need ballast. About ten tons."

"Mmmmmm," Phillips said. "That could be a problem. Did you check with *Canopus?*"

"Yes. They melted down all the lead they had for ammo."

"How about sandbags?" Phillips asked.

"That's an idea," Slack said. He turned to Bellinger. "Will you ask the Army if they can spare us sandbags? A lot of sandbags in a hurry?"

"Aye, aye," Bellinger said.

Bellinger trotted up to an Army command post near the head of the pier. He found an infantry major in charge of the area. He laughed when Bellinger asked where he might draw ten tons of sandbags.

"Sandbags are the most valuable commodity on the Rock, sailor," the major elaborated. "Worth their weight in gold."

Bellinger trotted back to report the bad news to Phillips and Slack. As they were discussing what to do now, the topside watch called out from the temporary land-phone installation near the brow. "Call for the Captain, Mister Phillips. You want to take it?"

Phillips went over the brow and answered the telephone.

"Captain Holmes?"

"No, this is the exec, Lieutenant Phillips."

"Phillips, this is General Southerland, Chief of Staff to General MacArthur."

"Yes sir, General. What can I do for you?"

"The general has a special request to ask of your captain. Will you have him report to General MacArthur's headquarters right away?"

"I certainly will, General."

"Thank you. Goodbye."

5

General Southerland ushered Holmes into MacArthur's office in a bay off the main tunnel. MacArthur, seated behind a desk, was working on a stack of papers and smoking a corncob pipe.

"Commander Holmes of *Swordray*," Southerland said.

MacArthur looked up, beaming. He rose and strode around the desk, hand extended. "God bless the submarine force Holmes," the General began. "The Navy has let me down, but, by God, you got through with food and ammo. In behalf of the entire garrison, I want to thank you and your crew from the bottom of my heart."

He shook hands warmly, then put his arm around Holmes' shoulder. "I'm putting you and every man on that boat in for a Silver Star. You've been magnificent, an example of courage for all the world to note and praise."

Holmes was rendered speechless by the effusiveness of the greeting. What they had brought in was insignificant. Certainly not deserving of a medal. An Army award at that! What complications that would cause in the Navy Department!

MacArthur returned to his desk and invited Holmes to sit. He went on, "When you get back to the rear area, I want you to tell them what a splendid job my troops are doing here against overwhelming odds. We've tactically reconsolidated our positions on the Bagac-Orion Line. An impregnable defense, Commander, An anvil against which Homma will smash his head to pieces. We have stopped him cold. Soon we shall break out, mount an offensive and drive him out of the Philippines or slaughter every one of his men. But tell them I need more of everything. Planes. Guns. Ammo. Food."

He went on in this vein for fifteen minutes. Holmes could scarcely believe his ears. What the General had to say bore little resemblence to the reality as Holmes knew it. But Holmes kept his council. No purpose would be served in challenging the General's view. It was obviously deep-seated, unchangeable.

Was this the favor the General wanted of Holmes? To carry back his hopelessly optimistic view? No. There was something else.

"Commander," MacArthur said, finally getting to the point. "I have a special request to ask of you. We have here in the tunnel the Philippine gold reserves. About sixteen million dollars in gold ingots. President Quezon has become a defeatist. He is quite anxious to have this gold shipped to the United States, so there's no possibility the Japs could get it. By any chance could you take it out for him?"

Again Holmes was stunned. He gulped and stammered. "I . . . I think . . . I'm sure we could, sir. How much does it weigh?"

"I don't know." He pressed a buzzer and General Southerland appeared immediately.

"How much does the gold weigh?"

"About ten tons, sir."

"Why that's perfect!" Holmes said. "Matter of fact, we've been looking for some ballast. The ingots could well serve that purpose." Gold ballast! It was incredible.

"Very well, Holmes," MacArthur said, rising. "President Quezon will be very grateful, I'm sure." He turned to Southerland. "Will you see it's delivered to the pier immediately?"

"Yes, sir," Southerland said, withdrawing.

"When you get to Java," MacArthur continued, "tell Admiral Hart to send me a thousand submarines full of food and ammo."

"Aye, aye, General. I'll deliver your message, sir."

MacArthur smiled and said, "Good luck, Holmes. Again, my thanks for a job well done. I wish the Navy had more people like you who are willing to run risks, to *fight*."

"Yes, sir," Holmes said. "And good luck to you, sir."

Back at *Swordray*, Holmes told Phillips, Slack and Bellinger the news. "You're not going to believe this, but I've solved our ballast problem. Or rather, MacArthur solved it for us. He's sending over ten tons of gold ingots."

"Well, how thoughtful," Phillips said sarcastically. "In payment for the food and ammo we brought?"

"No, it's true," Holmes said. He explained the request. Only then did they believe him.

6

The gold arrived two hours later, stacked in the bed of an ancient Ford truck, covered with a greasy tarpaulin. Behind that truck came another, full of armed Filipino soldiers. The trucks drove out on the pier, the soldiers deployed, weapons ready.

A civilian in a white suit and tie climbed out of the cab of the gold truck, clutching a sheaf of papers. He was obviously the man in charge. Phillips stepped forward, saluted and introduced himself. The man was Juan Ortega, Minister of Finance, Philippine Government.

"Will you please sign for this?" Ortega asked, offering the sheaf of papers.

Phillips looked at the papers. It was an inventory of the ingots. "Maybe I ought to have a look at it first," he said.

Ortega led Phillips to the rear of the truck and pulled back the tarpaulin. Phillips, Slack and Bellinger stared wide-eyed at the gleaming bars.

"Look at that!" Bellinger said. "Millions of bucks!"

"How much is one of those bars worth in U.S. currency?" Phillips asked Ortega.

"About thirty thousand dollars."

Phillips whistled. Then he said, "Before I sign, I'm going to count it. Bellinger, you're in charge of the count. Get a pencil and some paper and be very, very accurate because I'm going to count it again when we get back to Surabaya and unload it. Not that I wouldn't trust you like my brother. Hank, tell the Captain the gold's here. Then round up a twenty-man working party and form a bucket brigade. Load aft first, then forward. Better weigh one of these bars and get an exact figure. All right, on the double now, it's getting late."

During the counting and loading, Phillips tried to keep his mind off Anne. He engaged in small talk with Ortega. "How's President Quezon getting along?"

"Very bad," Ortega said. "He's a very sick man. Sick in the chest—tuberculosis—and sick in the heart."

"I can understand," Phillips said.

"Your President let him down," Ortega said. "He promised help and sends no help. Our troops are dying bravely by the thousands because your President said to stand and fight. And he sends no help."

"I'm afraid there is no way to send help now," Phillips said.

"I know," Ortega said. "It is all utter madness. Your President should release us from his commitment. Let the Philippines negotiate a separate peace with the Japanese. Both your Army and the Japanese Army should be withdrawn, the Filipino Army disbanded. We would become a neutral."

"Is that what your President wants to do?" Phillips asked.

"It is being discussed by the council," Ortega said. "It's one possibility—to stop the needless bloodshed."

"I doubt the Japs would buy it," Phillips said.

"Why not? We have nothing they want. No oil or rice."

"You have land for air bases and harbors for naval bases," Phillips said. "They won't give those up." The two men broke off the conversation, politely at odds.

When the loading was complete, Bellinger reported to Slack, "Five hundred and eighty-three bars. At thirty thousand a bar, that comes to seventeen million, four hundred ninety thousand dollars. Each bar weighs thirty-three pounds. That's a total of nineteen thousand, two hundred and thirty-nine pounds. Right at ten tons."

"Thanks, Tom," Slack said.

Phillips and Slack conferred, checking the papers. The Philippine inventory tallied exactly at five hundred and eighty-three bars. Phillips signed all five copies of the document. Ortega counter-signed one copy and gave it to Phillips. They shook hands.

"President Quezon thanks you deeply for this service," Ortega said.

"Tell him we're glad to do it," Phillips said.

"Till we meet again, then," Ortega said. "Goodbye and good luck."

Chapter Eight

1

Swordray left the Celebes Sea astern and nosed southward into Makassar Strait, the narrow body of water lying between Borneo and Celebes Island. Her destination was Surabaya, Java, about six hundred miles to the south. It would be a dangerous transit. The Japanese had overrun Borneo and Celebes several weeks past. Their planes and destroyers now patrolled the three-hundred-mile-long strait in force.

In spite of the patrols, Holmes decided to make the transit running on the surface. For one thing, there was not sufficient air in the boat to sustain one hundred and eleven men submerged. For another, they could travel an average of seven times faster on the diesels. He was anxious to reach Surabaya as quickly as possible. *Swordray* was running out of food.

Fred Bohlen had the first watch in the strait that morning, the eight-to-twelve. The lookouts had been doubled from two to four and Tom Bellinger, noted for his keen eyesight, was asked to remain on the bridge all day. Each man covered a sector of the horizon and sky with binoculars. In addition, the regular quartermaster of the watch, Les Reed, stood a high periscope watch in the conning tower. It was a clear, hot, tropical day. Visibility was excellent.

At 0921 hours—as Les Reed later logged it—Tom Bellinger's eye picked up an indefinable mote on the

121

horizon dead ahead. Or he *thought* he did. Looking intently at the spot again, he saw nothing. Nonetheless, he spoke into the intercom to Reed in the conning tower, "Les, check the horizon at zero zero zero relative."

Fred Bohlen, startled out of a reverie, swung his glasses dead ahead. "What is it?"

"Not sure," Bellinger said. "I thought I had something, but maybe I'm seeing things."

"Mast on the horizon dead ahead," the intercom barked. It was Les Reed.

"Inform the captain and exec," Bohlen said.

"Aye," Reed said curtly. He was clearly excited.

Holmes and Phillips appeared on the bridge a half a minute later. They examined the horizon with binoculars but they could see nothing.

"Aircraft coming in astern!" a lookout in the shears cried out. All hands were galvanized.

Bohlen looked aft with his binoculars to confirm the contact, then shouted, "Clear the bridge! Clear the bridge. Dive! Dive!"

The eight men on the bridge rushed for the hatch at once. The vents hissed open, the diesels shut down. Bohlen, the last man down, pulled the hatch shut by the lanyard; Bellinger dogged it tight. Reed lowered the periscope.

"One hundred fifty feet," Bohlen called out. "Rig for depth charge." They could hear the watertight doors between the compartments slamming shut. *Swordray* nosed down.

"What was the range?" Holmes said.

"Three or four miles," Bohlen responded.

The plane would be over them in one minute, Holmes estimated. By that time, they should be at eighty feet.

"What's the depth here?" Bohlen asked Reed.

Reed looked at the chart. "Should be three hundred feet," he said.

"Take a sounding," Bohlen ordered control.

They heard the "ping" of the fathometer. Control reported, "Two hundred fifty feet."

"Very well," Bohlen said.

Swordray continued down. Sixty feet. Seventy. Eighty.

Holmes kept his eye on the stopwatch. Fifty seconds. A damned fast dive, their best time yet.

"Blow negative," Bohlen said. "Take the angle off."

WHAM! WHAM!

The two bombs exploded off the starboard bow almost simultaneously. The noise was deafening, the shock on the hull severe. It skewed *Swordray* to port and down. It knocked all hands off their feet, shattered glass dials and gauges and raised clouds of dust and cork.

"One hundred fifty feet," control reported.

"Right full rudder," Bohlen ordered. "Ahead full."

Holmes nodded approvingly. Bohlen's quick maneuver would take *Swordray* away from the point of the dive—and the first two bombs.

"All compartments have reported damage," control reported. "Nothing worth mentioning."

"Very well," Bohlen said. "Rudder amidships."

Holmes, suddenly remembering his passengers, picked up the p.a. mike and spoke. "Attention all hands. This is the Captain. A Jap plane made a run on us. Sorry we didn't have time to warn you. There's no internal damage, nothing more to worry about. He may try another run if he has any more bombs, but we're deep now. He can't find us."

The plane dropped no more bombs. However, there was in fact, something more to worry about. The plane had missed, but what about that mast on the horizon? The pilot was sure to radio the ship that an American submarine was in the vicinity. If the ship turned out to be a destroyer . . .

Holmes turned to Bohlen, "I'll take the conn, Fred. Nice job." Then to Phillips, "Secure from depth charge. Station the tracking party." Then to the helmsman, "Come right to one eight zero." Then to the sonarman, "Search zero zero zero relative."

Bohlen took over the T.D.C.; Bill Nolan the hand-plot tracking table in the rear of the conning tower. Phillips stood by, overseeing both and also prepared to assist the Captain.

"Faint screws, zero zero zero," the sonarman reported.

"Fast or slow?" Phillips said.

"Can't tell yet for certain, sir," the sonarman said.

Five minutes later, he was certain. "Fast screws and low-scale pinging at zero zero zero." It was a destroyer. Bohlen and Nolan began the tracking.

"Periscope depth," Holmes ordered. *Swordray* came up smartly to sixty feet. "Up scope," Holmes said.

He first swung the periscope three hundred and sixty degrees, searching both water and sky. "No planes, nothing in sight," he said. "Put me on zero zero zero."

Phillips, watching the overhead azimuth, turned the periscope to the bearing. Holmes searched the bearing but he could not see the target.

"Down scope."

The orders from Wilkes had been explicit: *Swordray* was not to engage the enemy on the run *to* Corregidor. But he had said nothing about the return trip. Now, with a full load of torpedoes, there was no reason why they should not engage the enemy.

"How long since last look?" Holmes asked.

"Four and a half minutes," Bellinger said, glancing at the stopwatch.

"Up scope."

Holmes searched the bearing, shifting the scope to high power. He could faintly see a mast. "There she is!" he said. "Stand by. Mark! Down scope."

"Zero zero four," Phillips sang out. Bohlen cranked the bearing into the TDC.

"No range," Holmes said. "Just the tip of the mast." He turned to Bohlen. "As a guess, put the range at fifteen thousand yards." Bohlen cranked in the data. The TDC dial began to turn slowly.

Four minutes later, by the stop watch, Holmes said, "Up scope."

He again swept the horizon around, then settled on the oncoming target. "Lot closer. Mark bearing! Down scope. Belay that! I see another mast close aboard. Second target. Mark bearing! Down scope."

He turned to the sonarman. "Could you have two sets of screws on that bearing?"

"I was just going to report that, Captain," the sonarman replied. "That's affirmative. Both long-scale pinging."

"Humph," Holmes grunted, casting a glance at Phillips. "Two destroyers. Wonder what they're escorting?"

Phillips said nothing. He was marveling at the calmness of Holmes' periscope technique under pressure.

"Let's see if we can get a range this time," Holmes said. "Up scope. Mark bearing! She's coming on fast. Angle on the bow ten starboard. Use a masthead height of forty." He cranked the stadimeter handle on the side of the scope, splitting the distant image. "Mark range!"

Phillips interpolated and read the range from the table mounted on the periscope. "Nine five oh oh."

"Down scope."

"Was that a good range, Captain?" Bohlen said, cranking in the data.

"No," Holmes said.

"I have eleven one oh oh," Bohlen said.

"You're probably right," Holmes said. "Split the difference. Let's not rush this."

"Okay," Bohlen said. "I've got him on course zero ten zero, speed twenty, range about ten thousand."

"Okay," Holmes said. "Come right to two seven zero."

The enemy was heading due north. *Swordray* would dogleg west to avoid the destroyer screen. The maneuver would place *Swordray* sideways to the enemy sonar pings —offering the destroyers the largest possible target—but Holmes was sure they were too far away and going too fast to pick them up.

"Steady on two seven zero," the helmsman said.

"Captain," the sonarman said matter-of-factly, "I'm now picking up very heavy screws behind the destroyers. It's a battleship or carrier."

Holmes' heart shot to his throat. No boat had yet attacked a battleship or carrier. *Swordray* could be the first. What a feather for *Swordray!* What a morale booster for the home front!

"How long since the last look?"

"Two and a half minutes."

"Up scope. Put me on the bearing of the heavy screws."

He pressed his eye into the eyepiece and focused. There it was! A *Haruna* class battleship, perhaps *Haruna* herself. Fighting to stay calm, he said, "Battlewagon. Mark! Down scope."

A wave of excitement swept the conning tower, then, as word spread, the whole boat. The TDC and tracking party shifted to the new target, the battleship.

"Up scope," Holmes said.

"You might want to check for that plane again," Phillips reminded.

"Right," Holmes said, grabbing the scope, sweeping the sky. He stopped the scope and said, "Hold it! There's the plane. Low. Five hundred feet. Appears to be circling."

He turned the glass down to the horizon and continued the sweep. "Damn!" he cried. "That sonofabitch dropped a smoke flare. Mark! That's the flare. Down scope."

A dead silence fell over the conning tower. Presently Holmes broke it. "The flare's aft, right on our track. He's been tailing us. He can see us in this clear water at periscope depth. One more look and let's go deep. Up scope. Put me on the destroyers."

Phillips turned the scope to the last bearing. "They've zigged toward!" Holmes said. "Mark! Down scope."

"Destroyers speeding up," the sonarman reported.

"Very well," Holmes said. "Dammit! Two hundred feet. Take a sounding."

Swordray eased down into deeper water, far below periscope depth. For the time being, they would depend on the sonarman's bearings on the destroyers, and his estimates of the ranges. They would not themselves ping on the destroyers because their ping could be heard and would give away their position.

Once again Holmes picked up the p.a. mike. "All hands, this is the Captain again. The plane is still with us and has vectored in two destroyers. We will evade them, if at all possible. The destroyers are escorting a *Haruna* class battleship. That's our target. We are going to battle stations. All passengers will please climb into empty bunks and make yourselves comfortable."

He said to Phillips, "Go to battle stations."

Phillips pressed the alarm. It gonged softly throughout the boat.

"Battle stations manned and ready," Phillips reported a moment later.

"Very well," Holmes said. "Rig for depth charge."

"Aye, aye." Phillips passed the word on the p.a. Again the watertight doors slammed shut.

"Two hundred feet," control reported.

A head appeared in the control room hatch. It was Lieutenant Commander Beale, commanding officer of the Corregidor evacuees—the mysterious radio communications group. He said, "Captain, may I see you privately for a minute?"

Holmes looked down at the man, thunderstruck. "I'm afraid we're busy," he said curtly.

"This is urgent," Beale insisted. "I *must* talk to you now."

"It *better* be urgent," Holmes said. "Take the conn, George. I'll be right back."

They went to Holmes' cabin and sat down. Beale said, "Captain, I must ask you to break off this attack and do everything in your power to evade the enemy."

"*What?* Are you mad?" Holmes cried, jumping up. "Go get in a bunk. I've got work to do."

Beale stood up and said, "In the best interest of the country, I cannot permit you to risk the loss—or capture —of my men."

Holmes stared at Beale. "Don't you know there's a war on, buddy? There's a battlewagon up there and we've got a chance to get it."

He turned to leave. Beale grabbed him by the shirt sleeve and said, "No! My men are more valuable to the war effort than sinking that battleship."

"Take your hands off me," Holmes said harshly.

Beale did not let go. "It is a violation of security to tell you this, but I see I must. My men—this unit—are Japanese codebreakers."

Holmes was stunned. He had heard that the U.S. Navy had broken the Japanese naval codes. But he had assumed the codebreakers were based in Washington, not Corregidor. He was momentarily speechless.

"We represent one-third of the Navy's entire code-breaking capability," Beale said. "That's why CNO ordered us evacuated. It's absolutely vital that this unit be delivered safely to a rear area. If we should be lost here in this shallow water, they could salvage the boat. They would find our decoding gear. That would tell them that their codes were compromised and they would change the codes. And that would be a greater setback to the Navy than Pearl Harbor. A real disaster."

"I see," Holmes said, nodding. Beale was absolutely correct. The codebreaking was a priceless asset, a secret to be protected at all costs. Concealing his disappointment, he went on, "All right, Beale, we'll do our best to evade and get you to Surabaya."

Holmes returned to the conning tower and spoke to the men, "For reasons I cannot explain, I'm aborting the attack. Let's do our damnedest to get out of here."

They stared at him in disbelief.

2

"Ahead two-thirds," Holmes said.

A steady stream of bearings and estimated ranges on the destroyers came from the sonarman. Bohlen and Nolan used these for tracking. The tracks showed the destroyers had changed course to northwest and were relentlessly closing in on *Swordray*.

"Come right to zero nine zero," Holmes said. He would reverse course, run the other way to throw them off. The maneuver would again expose the full length of *Swordray*—three hundred and eleven feet of steel—to their sonar.

"Ahead full." This to speed up *Swordray*'s swing.

"Range five oh oh oh," sonar reported. Two and a half miles. "They're slowing down, Captain."

"Are they turning?"

"They may be."

Holmes said to Phillips, "Are they mind readers?"

Phillips shrugged and said, "It must be the first team."

"Ahead flank," Holmes said, hastening the turn still more. "Let's run under them. Right full rudder. Steady on one one five."

It was a standard, much-rehearsed evasion tactic. By turning directly toward the pursuers, *Swordray* presented the smallest silhouette, and forced their sonar to listen through the turbulence of their own bow waves.

"Steady on one one five," the helmsman said.

"Ahead two-thirds," Holmes said. They could not afford to run at flank speed long. Continuous running at flank speed would drain the battery dry in one hour. From now on, conserving the battery would be primary.

"Range two oh oh oh."

The pursuers and the pursued—two hundred feet below—were now nose to nose and closing fast.

"Short-scale pinging, Captain!" the sonarman said in an urgent tone. "They've got us, Captain."

"Ahead one-third," Holmes said. "Rig for silent running."

Every piece of machinery on *Swordray* except the propulsion motors was shut down. That included the air conditioners and ventilation blowers which kept the air cool and circulating. Immediately they felt the heat rising in the conning tower. Very quickly they were bathed in sweat.

"Range one five oh oh."

Sweat ran down Bellinger's arm onto his hand and dampened the deck log in which he was noting—in his own shorthand—every detail of the encounter with the enemy. He leaned down the hatch to control and stage-whispered, "Send up some towels."

"The port destroyer is speeding up, Captain. Range one oh oh oh. I think he's making a run."

"Very well," Holmes said. "Two hundred thirty feet."

They planed down to within twenty feet of the bottom. They could hear the fast screws through the hull now. Holmes spoke quietly on the p.a. "This is the captain. We may be getting some depth charges, men. Passengers please remain in the bunks. Thank you."

"He's dropping!" sonar reported. "Rigging in sound heads." The sonarman jerked off his sweaty, padded earphones and looked directly up. The others followed his gaze, waiting tensely.

WHAM. WHAM. WHAM. WHAM. WHAM. WHAM.

The depth charges exploded above them with ear-splitting ferocity. The force of the explosions smashed *Swordray* to the bottom. Her nose dug into the mud, stopping the boat with a jolt that threw everybody forward.

"All back full," Holmes said. "All compartments report damage."

WHAM. WHAM. WHAM. WHAM. WHAM. WHAM.

These, too, exploded above them with violent force. Again *Swordray* was smashed into the muddy bottom.

"All stop," Holmes said. "Report damage."

WHAM. WHAM. WHAM. WHAM. WHAM. WHAM.

Again the explosions were above them. Why weren't they setting them to explode deeper? Holmes wondered. Thank God they were not.

The screws grew fainter as the destroyers pulled off to reload depth-charge racks and prepare for another run. They could now hear the heavier screws of the battleship through the hull. The damage reports poured in. Minor leaks. Valves unseated. Electrical circuits shorted out. Nothing serious.

Soaked with sweat, Holmes made a sudden decision. "Ahead emergency. Left full rudder. Rig out the sound heads. Periscope depth."

He turned to Phillips. "We won't have a snowball's chance in hell if we just sit here. They've got us dead to rights. The only chance we have is to fight our way out. Make ready the forward tubes. We'll set up on both targets at once. Fire three fish at each, down-the-throat."

"Aye, aye, Captain," Phillips said. "Now you're talking."

When *Swordray* reached periscope depth, Holmes squatted on the deck to grab the handles so that they would expose minimum periscope. He walked the scope around. The battleship was close and massive. He could see sailors on her deck madly pointing toward the periscope. He went on around the horizon to the two destroyers. "All right. Here they are. Target one. Bearing! Mark! Angle on the bow five port." He split the image. "Range. Mark!" He shifted the scope slightly. "Target two.

Bearing! Mark! Range! Mark! Angle on the bow twenty starboard. Down scope."

Bohlen and Nolan quickly set up the new plots. Holmes made three more quick periscope observations to give them more precise firing data. On the last, he said, "Target one is commencing run. Angle on the bow zero."

"Forward tubes ready," Phillips reported.

"Very well," Holmes said. "Ahead one-third. Open the outer doors. This will be a shooting observation on target one."

As the scope came up, he said to Phillips, "Set the torpedo depth at six feet. To hell with the magnetic exploders. We'll shoot to hit."

"Six feet, sir?" Phillips challenged, knowing full well this was going to cost Holmes a court-martial.

"Six feet," Holmes said, grabbing the scope handles.

"Aye, aye, sir."

The destroyer was coming dead on at high speed, making smoke. Holmes could see white-uniformed sailors gesticulating at the periscope from the forward deck and bridge. "Come on, you slant-eyed bastards," he said to himself. "Prepare to join your ancestors."

"Mark bearing! Mark range! Angle on the bow zero. Down scope."

Bohlen cranked in the final data and reported, "Solution light. Fire anytime, Captain."

"Fire one! Fire two! Fire three!" Holmes intoned calmly. Then, "Up scope."

To himself, he said a prayer that the torpedoes would function. A down-the-throat shot at an oncoming destroyer was the riskiest shot of all, to be made only in desperation. The theory—or hope—was the destroyer skipper would see the torpedoes coming dead on at his ship, panic, and turn port or starboard to avoid them and thereby catch a torpedo broadside. But what if he failed to follow the theory and did not turn? Kept coming straight on and "combing" the torpedoes? The chances of a hit on his thin, bow-on silhouette were remote. Moreover, the torpedo wakes gave him a precise position on the submarine at periscope depth. He could not miss with his depth charges.

Holmes could see the steamy, bubbly wakes of the torpedoes streaking toward the onrushing destroyer. So far, so good. He said, "All fish running hot, straight and normal."

He left the scope up. There was no point now in concealing it. The destroyer knew they had to be at periscope depth and exactly where they were.

"He zigged to port!" Holmes exclaimed. They had taken the bait. He watched almost hypnotized as the destroyer heeled to starboard in a wide sweeping turn. Number three torpedo, he saw, was going to catch her amidships.

He watched the geyser of water rise along the waterline, then a massive eruption of flames. Seconds later, they heard the explosion in the conning tower. Holmes saw the destroyer rise, back broken, in an inverted V. It broke in half and the two sections plunged at once beneath the sea.

"My God!" he said aloud. "We got her. She's gone."

There was dead silence for a moment in the conning tower, then Bellinger let go with a bellow, *"Goddamn! That's great!"*

Holmes followed the wakes of the other two torpedoes, number one and number two. They had missed when the destroyer turned. Then he saw the massive battleship again. She was moving at high speed, directly into the track of the torpedoes. "By God," he shouted, "one and two are going to hit the battlewagon."

They did. Both in her bow. He saw the geysers of water, then flames at the waterline, then they heard two explosions in the conning tower. "Two hits!" Holmes marveled. "What luck!"

He saw the battleship abruptly slowing down. Her bow wave diminished rapidly, her ensign began to flap idly.

"Captain," Phillips reminded, "the other destroyer?"

"Right," said Holmes, spinning the scope around. "Here she is. Stand by. Mark bearing! Mark range! Angle on the bow forty port."

"Forty port?" Bohlen questioned.

Holmes looked again. "Yes. Forty port."

"Four six oh oh," Phillips reported. "Was that a good range, Captain?"

"Yes," Holmes said, putting the cross hairs on the destroyer.

"What's he *doing?*" Phillips demanded impatiently.

"He's not doing anything," Holmes said. "He's slowing down. He's going toward the battleship. He's making signals to the battleship. I don't think he's going to make a run on us. Goddamn! Maybe he's lost his taste for a fight."

"You want to set up on the wagon?" Phillips prodded.

Holmes examined the battleship. He could see smoke and flame forward and damage control parties rushing about. But she could not be seriously damaged. Her side armor plate would protect her from torpedoes set to run at six feet. However, they had done *some* damage. She was barely creeping along, perhaps to prevent flooding forward. The destroyer was positioning herself along the battleship, on *Swordray*'s side. A shield.

It occurred to Holmes that here was a priceless opportunity to conduct a "live" torpedo test on a real target. The destroyer had obviously given up the fight. The plane, probably low on fuel, had gone. There would be no danger to the codebreakers. It was almost a laboratory setup.

Still glued to the periscope, he said to Phillips, "Let's see if these magnetic exploders will work on a battleship as designed. Set up on the battleship. Mark bearing! Mark range! Angle on the bow ninety port. Zero gyro angle. All stop. We'll fire four, five and six. Depth set thirty feet."

He took his time. They eased in to nine hundred yards range, leaving the periscope up. When the fire control solution was as perfect as they could get it, Holmes said, "Fire four!"

He watched the torpedo wake streak toward the battleship. It was a perfect shot. It passed beneath the shallow-draft destroyer. But beyond, there was no explosion. Nothing at all.

"Fire five," Holmes said. A perfect shot. No explosion.

"Fire six," Holmes said. Another perfect shot. No explosion.

"Well, shit!" Phillips said. "If that doesn't prove it, nothing does."

"Down scope," Holmes said. "Come right to one eight zero. Ahead two-thirds. Secure from battle stations. Set the regular watch."

Chapter Nine

1

Swordray took the Dutch pilot aboard in Bunda Roads at the mouth of Surabaya Harbor. He was a stolid man who wore a plaid cap and smoked a pipe.

"Is it true that Singapore has fallen?" Holmes asked after they had settled in on the bridge. They had heard the "news" on Tokyo Rose, but had no official confirmation.

"Yes," the Dutchman said. "We heard it on BBC last night. Shocking. This morning the Japs parachuted into Sumatra—virtually unopposed. They've begun landing on Timor."

Timor lay to the east of Java along the Malaya Barrier; Sumatra to the west. Java was now caught in a pincer movement.

"I expect they'll be here any day now," the pilot said, smacking the pipe in the palm of his hand. Then to the intercom, "Steer two nine one."

"What's left of the Asiatic Fleet surface force?" Holmes said.

"Well, *Marblehead* took a mauling. Miracle she didn't sink. *Boise* ran aground and severely damaged her bottom. You've not got much left except your heavy cruiser *Houston*—and she's been damaged—our cruiser *De Ruyter* and a half-dozen destroyers. We won't stop the Japs with that line up, I'm afraid. If Java is to be saved, it's up to you submariners. . . . Helmsman, steer three zero zero."

Holmes nodded silently at the bad news. They had heard it all on Tokyo Rose, bit by bit. She had said

Japanese troops would soon attack Java. There was no way the sub force could stop them.

"Is *Holland* here?" he asked.

"No," the pilot said. "She's down on the south coast at Tjilatjap. She couldn't survive here. The Jap bombers come over every day promptly at noon."

"You mean they've been *bombing* Surabaya?" Holmes asked, astonished.

"Since February third," the pilot said.

"Then why were *we* ordered here?" Holmes said.

"You'll be safe in our navy yard," the pilot said. "Heavy anti-aircraft batteries. Good camouflage. You'll find a number of your boats in refit here."

The pilot now gave his full attention to conning *Swordray* up the channel into the harbor. In the outer mooring areas there were a half-dozen badly bombed ships resting on the bottom. Tom Bellinger fixed his binoculars on one that looked familiar. It was *Piet Heyn*, sunk to her promenade deck. Her bridge was a mass of twisted wreckage. And where was Rosaria? Singapore? Here?

"Do you know where I can find Commodore Wilkes?" Holmes asked the pilot as they approached the inner harbor.

"He's at the base," the pilot said. "The whole submarine staff. Though for how long, I can't say."

There were six U.S. fleet boats and one S-boat undergoing refit in the small yard. They were moored at two piers and concealed beneath a giant camouflaged "roof." The pilot eased *Swordray* beneath the roof and nested her alongside Roland Pryce's *Spearfish*. No one was there to meet the boat. Soon after the brow went over, a messenger arrived from Wilkes' office summoning Holmes and Phillips.

The commodore had set up quarters in what had formerly been the Dutch yard captain's office. Wilkes, Fife and Murray were meeting when Holmes and Phillips arrived. The three senior officers looked like men who had not slept in weeks. Wilkes and Fife were, as usual, aloof and chilly; Murray was his same cheery self. At Wilkes' direction, the group took seats at a conference table.

"Here is my patrol report," Holmes said, handing Wilkes a heavy sealed manila envelope.

"The mission was successful?" Wilkes asked. "You delivered the food and ammo?"

"Yes," Holmes said. "General MacArthur extends his personal thanks to Admiral Hart and all others concerned. He said, 'Send me a thousand submarines full of food and ammo.' "

"Pompous ass," Wilkes snorted.

Holmes paused a moment, then resumed, "On the way out, we picked up the spare parts from *Canopus* and eighteen torpedoes." He paused again, selecting his words carefully. "In addition, we evacuated fifty-one naval personnel. . . ."

"You *what?*" Wilkes shouted. "You endangered your boat with a mob like that?"

"Sir, at no time did the passengers present a problem in terms of operational or combat effectiveness. We ran out of food, but that was no problem. Most of my men should be on diets anyway."

The feeble attempt at humor fell flat. Wilkes said, "You should be court-martialed for that, Holmes."

"Commodore," Holmes said, suppressing a rising anger, "I was ordered by Commander Sackett to evacuate those personnel. He had orders from CNO to get them out on the next boat calling at Corregidor."

"CNO orders?" Wilkes echoed.

"Yes, sir," Holmes said.

"Who are they?" Wilkes demanded.

"A radio communications group," Holmes said. "Japanese codebreakers."

Phillips was thunderstruck. Now he understood why Holmes had broken off the initial attack on the battleship.

Wilkes turned to Fife. "See that they are evacuated at once to Australia. Send them overland to Tjilatjap to *Holland.* Keep CNO informed."

Fife jotted these instructions on a tablet.

"There is something else," Holmes resumed. "General MacArthur, in behalf of President Quezon, requested that we take out the Philippine Government gold reserves. Seventeen million dollars in gold ingots. As it happened, we needed ten tons of ballast. The gold fit the bill perfectly."

The three senior men stared at Holmes in astonishment. Wilkes said, "You mean to tell me you've got seventeen million dollars in gold in your bilges?"

"Yes, sir," Holmes said without changing expression.

Murray's face lit up. He said to Wilkes, "John, that's one hell of a newspaper story. Sub sneaks the Philippine gold right out from under the Jap noses! A hell of a story." He turned to Holmes. "Congratulations."

"Yes," Wilkes agreed. "We could release that, I guess."

"It would make a better story than 'Sturgeon no longer virgin,'" Murray said.

"Any more goodies up your sleeve?" Wilkes said.

"We got two hits on a *Haruna*-class battleship," Holmes said in a deliberate, low-key voice. "And we sank a destroyer."

"*What?*" Wilkes cried. "When? Where?"

"Makassar Strait," Holmes replied. "Two days ago."

"Well, man, go on," Wilkes said impatiently. "Go on. Give us the details."

"You're not going to like it, Commodore," Holmes said. "I want to preface this by saying I was deliberately insubordinate. I violated your specific orders on the depth setting of the torpedoes."

Wilkes fixed Holmes with an icy stare. "Go on. Lay it out."

For the next fifteen minutes, Holmes spelled out the details of the attack. Phillips assisted by producing a track chart and other technical details. Wilkes, Fife and Murray listened transfixed.

"So there it is, sir," Holmes concluded. "Three hits with a six-foot depth setting; no hits from three fish set at thirty feet against a virtually immobile battleship. I believe, sir, these results demand a live, controlled test of the torpedoes."

Wilkes drummed a pencil on the top of the table, staring out the window. Then he said to Phillips, "Did you see the tin can sink?"

"No, sir," Phillips.

"There wasn't time for him to take a good look," Holmes said. "She blew in half and went straight down."

"How about the hits on the battleship?" Wilkes said to Phillips.

"No, sir."

Wilkes stared at Holmes for a moment, then said, "I'm sorry, but I can't accept that report. I doubt you got those hits with those depth settings."

"I can assure you, sir, the tin can sank," Holmes said, again suppressing anger.

"Nonetheless, I cannot credit it," Wilkes said. "Nor the hits on the battleship. You don't know for sure they were hits. They could have been end-of-the-run self-detonations."

"No, sir," Holmes said firmly. "They were hits. I saw the geysers at the waterline. And the flames and damage control parties on deck."

Wilkes terminated the discussion with further instructions to Fife. "Send the gold to *Holland* with the code-breakers. Be sure it's securely guarded."

Again, Fife jotted notes on the tablet.

Wilkes turned to Holmes. "Lou Shane on *Shark* will be in port about a week. *Shark* is feeling her age. She's in terrible shape, needs extensive refitting. Shane will relieve you on *Swordray*. You will temporarily command *Shark* during the refit until I can find a qualified skipper."

"But, sir. . ." Phillips attempted.

"Shut up, George," Holmes said sternly.

For the first time since Holmes had known him, Sunshine Murray's face was clouded.

Wilkes said to Murray, "On second thought, don't release the gold story. That is all, gentlemen."

2

Tom Bellinger was astonished to hear a voice on the p.a. system exclaim joyously, "Mail call! Mail call topside." They had not had mail since before the war started.

He joined the rush topside. Les Reed was distributing the little packets of letters. "Allen . . . Anderson . . . Armstrong . . . Bellinger . . ."

Bellinger received two letters, both from his mother, one written before the war, one after—on Christmas Day. He read them in sequence. There was no real news. Everything was fine, his father was eighty-five percent recovered from his stroke. His sister had taken a job as a riveter in the Mare Island shipyard. She hoped he was safe, etc.

Jack Lyons came over, folding a letter, putting it in his dungaree shirt pocket. "You hitting the beach?" he asked.

"Yes," Bellinger said. "Rosaria might be here. I'm going to look for her."

"I'll keep you company."

They dressed in whites and caught a taxi at the main gate. "Customs and Immigration," Bellinger directed.

The chief of Customs and Immigration turned out to be a fat, jolly, helpful man. He found Rosaria Martinez in his files. She had arrived from Singapore on the *S.S. Piet Heyn*, local address the Royal Arms Hotel. But that had been demolished in the bombings. There was no record of her leaving Java. "However," he said, "you must understand our records are no longer reliable. People are fleeing in small boats by the hundreds without going through immigration."

"Well, thanks a lot," Bellinger said.

"You're more than welcome," he said. "You men are submariners, I see. It's all up to you. Can you stop them?"

"We're going to give it a hell of a try," Bellinger said.

"Good luck."

They took another cab to the waterfront brothel and bar district. They called at five whorehouses. No one had ever heard of Rosaria Martinez; nor had anyone seen a woman who answered her description. Bellinger was not really surprised. The area was too raunchy for Rosaria.

They taxied on, querying the room clerks at the six largest hotels. No one named Rosaria Martinez had registered at any of the hotels.

"Any ideas?" Bellinger said to Lyons when they left the last hotel.

"How about the police?"

"All right."

The Chief of Police found a record. One Rosaria Martinez, forty-five years old, home address 69 Calle d'Oro, Manila, had, on January 31, 1942, been assaulted by an unknown thief and robbed of two hundred Dutch guilders. She had been found lying unconscious in the park by a constable. Local address, the East Indies Inn.

They took yet another taxi to the inn. It was a clean, moderately-priced establishment back near the main gate of the Navy base. The desk clerk was a suspicious, surly Chinese.

"Who wants to know?" he snarled.

"I'm an old friend of hers," Bellinger said. "I owe her money. I want to pay her back."

The clerk looked sharply at Bellinger, then he said, "She's gone. Checked out. She could have used the money. She had to pay her bill with her diamond earrings."

"Do you know where she went?"

"Where everybody's going," the clerk answered. "Australia."

"How?"

"She got passage on a sampan."

"When?"

"About five—six days ago."

"Was she well?"

"Considering she was beaten and robbed," the clerk said.

"I heard," Bellinger said.

"Did she really own a beauty parlor in Manila?" the clerk asked, eyes narrowing.

"I'll say she did," Bellinger replied. "The best in the city."

"I didn't believe her."

There was a bar, The Anchor to Windward, off the foyer. It was crowded with noisy sailors on liberty. They found two seats at the bar and ordered bourbon.

"Remarkable gal," Lyons said.

"Resourceful," Bellinger said. "Knows how to take care of herself." He took a sip of his drink and said, "Where the hell did they dig up our mail?"

"The guy who brought it said *Holland* got it in Australia. Darwin."

"Good old *Holland*," Bellinger said. Then, carefully, "What's the news from home?"

"Bad," he said.

Lyons took out the folded letter and gave it to Bellinger to read. "She wants a divorce," he said gloomily.

Bellinger scanned the letter. She had fallen in love with an Air Corps sergeant. "Give her the divorce," he said, returning the letter. "She's been screwing you long enough. Deep-six her."

"I think I will."

"Don't *think*, Jack. Do it."

"I'm worried about the kids."

"They'll make out."

"I want to think on it some."

"You figure long, you figure wrong," Bellinger said. "Well, kiss my ass, look who's here!"

It was an old friend of both of theirs, Chief Quartermaster Dan Parker from *Seadragon*. They shook hands warmly.

"I heard you got seventeen million bucks in your bilges," Parker said. "How about lending me a couple of thou?"

"Sure," Bellinger said. "Come on by. The Old Man's lending it out at twenty-five percent interest. Draw all you want."

"Is it really true?" Parker said. "You brought out the gold?"

"It's true," Bellinger nodded.

"What a story!" Parker said. "How's old Dugout Doug?"

"He sent you his best," Bellinger replied.

"How much longer can he hold out?"

"Not long," Bellinger said. "A few weeks at most."

Lyons said to Parker, "We heard your pharmacist's mate performed an appendectomy with bent spoons. Is that true?"

"Yup," Parker said. He added, "Boy did Wilkes chew out the Old Man for that! He was lucky he didn't get relieved. Then Wilkes turns right around and crows about it in a publicity release. Strange bird, the Commodore."

"How many skippers has he canned so far?" Bellinger asked.

"Seven," Parker said. "If you include yours."

"He got the shaft," Bellinger said defensively. "He's a damned good man."

"A fish with his mouth open always gets caught," Parker said.

"So what are *you* guys doing about your torpedoes?" Bellinger asked.

"Setting them shallow," Parker answered. "But in the official reports, we put thirty or forty feet."

"Any hits?"

"Yes, we got a big transport."

"What was your depth setting?"

"Ten feet."

"We used six. Sank a tin can and got two hits on a battlewagon."

"No shit?" Parker said, much impressed. "A battle-wagon?"

"No shit."

They fell silent a moment, then Lyons started up angrily, "This is a hell of a way to fight a fucking war. Lying in the official reports! The Commodore's a pig-headed asshole. He ought to be relieved. I've a good mind to march right down there and kick him in the ass!"

"Better have another drink first, Jack," Parker said. "You kick him in the ass, it'll be about twenty years in Portsmouth before you get another."

An SP hurried into the bar, shouting, "Knock it off! Knock it off!" The chatter died instantly.

"All hands report to their ships on the double! Commodore's orders."

The Java invasion force had been sighted by a U.S. Navy patrol plane. All naval vessels in the Java area steamed out to engage it—including *Swordray* with Holmes still temporarily in command.

3

Swordray patrolled the lower end of Makassar Strait where the Java invasion force had first been sighted. The other boats patrolled on a scouting line to the east and west of her. It was a clear moonless night; visibility was excellent.

A radio message arrived from Wilkes at 2330:

ALLIED CRUISERS HOUSTON, PERTH AND DERUYTER PLUS DESTROYER SCREEN VALIANTLY ENGAGED AN OVERWHELMINGLY SUPERIOR ENEMY TASK FORCE TODAY JAVA SEA. DERUYTER AND FOUR DESTROYERS LOST. ALL SUBMARINES THIS COMMAND WILL DO UTMOST TO SEEK OUT ENEMY TASK FORCE AND ATTACK.

Holmes passed the message to Phillips without comment. Phillips scanned the message and said, "That pretty much leaves it up to us."

"And we're not going to do any good with the standing orders on torpedo depth settings," Holmes said with a weary sigh.

The radioman, Art Evans, rapped urgently on the bulkhead, then entered the wardroom and said, "*Salmon*'s found the task force, Captain." He handed Holmes the message and withdrew.

Holmes and Phillips eagerly bent over Gene McKinney's contact report. He had spotted the main invasion force: six battleships, nine heavy cruisers and twenty destroyers escorting an armada of an estimated one hundred troop transports. Course, due south—to Java.

"By God!" Holmes said, quickly plotting the coordinates on a chart. "They're not more than fifty miles from here. Let's go!"

They hurried to the bridge. Bill Nolan had the deck. He had already turned *Swordray* toward the reported position of the enemy fleet. Holmes said, "I'll take the conn, Bill."

"Aye, sir," Nolan said.

"All ahead flank," Holmes said to the intercom. "Ask maneuvering to give us every turn they can squeeze out."

Swordray, sped southwest in a moderate sea, decks vibrating from the strain of maximum power. "Twenty point four knots," the intercom reported.

Holmes said to Phillips, "A two-and-a-half hour run at this speed. How about refining our interception point? Assume an enemy speed of twelve knots, course due south."

"Yes, sir, Captain," Phillips said, immediately dropping down the hatch. Two minutes later he spoke on the intercom. "Captain, recommend course two two zero."

"Make it so," Holmes replied. "Tell the forward and after torpedo rooms to recheck every torpedo in the tubes."

"Aye."

A moment later, Phillips said on the intercom, "Captain, urgent priority message from Wilkes. All submariners directed to intercept enemy and—the Commodore says—attack, attack, attack."

"Very well," Holmes said.

Two hours later—at 0200—Phillips came to the bridge and reported, "Captain, I estimate it's about ten miles to the intercept point. Recommend we go to battle stations."

"Go to battle stations," Holmes said quietly.

Henry Slack and Tom Bellinger instantly came to the bridge. Slack relieved Nolan; Bellinger relieved the duty quartermaster. Holmes said to Phillips, Slack and Bellinger, "The U-boats in the Atlantic have done pretty well with the night surface attack. There's no moon. Why don't we give it a try?"

The night surface attack—using *Swordray* like a PT boat—was not recommended procedure, especially against an enemy task force. It would be hazardous in the extreme. But the three men nodded approval.

Holmes startled them again. "And we'll go after the troop transports, not the warships. We're not going to sink any capital ships with these lousy torpedoes, but we might get another transport. Every Jap soldier we can stop from reaching that beach will make the job easier for the defenders."

"The Commodore won't like that," Phillips cautioned.

"I don't think the Commodore knows how to fight a submarine war," Holmes said quietly but determinedly. "I'll take the full responsibility."

"Gunfire on the horizon!" Ed Strong, a battle stations lookout, cried from his perch in the periscope shears. "Zero one zero."

Instantly, all on the bridge fixed binoculars on the bearing. The distant gunfire was continuous. "That's the task force," Holmes said. He adjusted *Swordray*'s course, heading directly toward the flashes.

The intercom spoke, "Intercepted message from *Perch* to the Commodore, Captain. She has found and engaged the enemy. Under severe counterfire."

"Very well," Holmes said.

"*Salmon* also engaging task force."

"Very well," Holmes repeated.

That was good news for *Swordray,* Holmes judged. *Perch* and *Salmon* would keep the task force occupied, perhaps leaving the transports unguarded.

"I'll get below and set up the tracking party, Captain," Phillips said.

"Very well, George."

"Good hunting," Phillips said, ducking below.

The intense naval gunfire on the horizon drew ever closer. Above the roar of *Swordray*'s diesels, those on the bridge could now hear the deep rumbling of the guns.

Holmes estimated that the troop transports would be coming along behind the task force and adjusted the intercept course accordingly. At 0241—as Bellinger logged it—lookout Ed Strong again cried out, "Transports—bearing three zero zero."

"Good work, Strong," Holmes sang out. He climbed up into the shears and fixed his binoculars on the bearing. He could see them clearly. Ship after ship after ship, apparently unguarded by escorts. He counted thirty before giving up and dropping back to the bridge.

"George, we've got the transports in sight," Holmes

said to the intercom. "Stand by for observations. Mark range! Mark bearing!"

The fire control and tracking parties in the conning tower absorbed the flow of data from the bridge. Holmes said, "George, the ships are steaming in two long columns. No escorts in sight. I'm going to go right down between the columns. We'll set up on the first four ships in line. Fire three bow tubes each at the first ship in either column, then two stern tubes each at the second ships in either column. Then we'll pull off and reload the tubes and see if we can get in a second attack."

Phillips repeated the attack plan word for word. It was the standard text-book solution—for a submerged periscope attack. He added, "Depth setting, Captain?"

"Ten feet."

"Ten feet, aye."

"Sir," Bellinger said, "how do you want that last order logged?"

"Ten feet."

"I'm starting our run in now, George," Holmes said quietly into the intercom. "Left full rudder."

Swordray made a wide sweeping turn, pulling ahead of the slow-moving transports. Holmes then maneuvered until *Swordray* was nose-to-nose with the two oncoming columns. In his calm voice, he fed continuous data to the conning tower.

"Distance to the track one-five-oh-oh," Phillips reported. "We have a solution on TDC. Recommend you shoot now, Captain."

"Very well," Holmes said. "Ahead two-thirds. Open the outer doors."

Swordray abruptly slowed to surface torpedo firing speed.

"Twelve knots," Phillips said.

"Fire one, two and three," Holmes said. "Ten second intervals."

The first torpedo swished from the forward tube. The second and third followed at ten-second intervals. Holmes watched their bubbly wakes with his binoculars. They appeared to be running hot, straight and normal, toward the transport leading the left-hand column.

"Fire four, five and six," Holmes ordered. "Ten-second intervals."

Holmes still had his binoculars on the first three torpedoes. The second in line suddenly rose to the surface. "Number two broached!" he spoke into the intercom. "Running erratic."

The torpedo porpoised crazily on the surface, struck a wave head-on and slewed far off course. Holmes saw instantly that its rudder had jammed full port. It was now commencing a wide circular turn to port, coming back toward *Swordray*.

"Circular run," Holmes said into the intercom.

Swordray was now almost abreast of the lead ships in both columns, commencing her run down the sea alley between them. The columns were only a thousand yards apart, leaving *Swordray* little room for sideway maneuver.

"Check fire," Holmes said, binoculars glued to the circling torpedo. "All ahead flank."

At that instant, the first torpedo hit the left-hand transport in the port bow. By then, she was only 500 yards off *Swordray*'s port beam. The torpedo evidently hit an ammo locker; the explosion was mind-numbing. Holmes saw the entire port side of the ship blow away. The shock wave reeled *Swordray* sharply to starboard, forcing those on the bridge to hang on. The transport went straight down, bow-first, like a huge ungainly submarine.

Holmes took in the scene in a split-second. Then he retrained his binoculars on the oncoming erratic torpedo. To evade it, Holmes would make a quick turn to port, thus paralleling the track of the torpedo on the opposite course. Suddenly, he was blinded by a powerful searchlight from the second target—the lead ship in the starboard column.

"They see us, George," Holmes spoke to the intercom. "Helmsman, stand by for a port turn."

Temporarily blinded, Holmes could only guess at the proper moment to turn. If he guessed wrong . . .

"Incoming mail!" Bellinger shouted.

He had been watching the beam of the lead transport's blinding searchlight. Suddenly he saw the muzzle blast of the stern gun. The shell wooshed over *Swordray*'s bridge.

"Left full rudder," Holmes said, devoutly hoping his guess was good. *Swordray* turned sharply to port.

"There it is!" Slack cried out, pointing to the port side.

"Rudder amidships!" Holmes cried.

The steaming torpedo wake passed down the port side of *Swordray*, fifteen feet off the saddle tanks. At that instant, the fourth torpedo slammed into the second target. Her searchlight went out and the stern gun fell silent.

"Hit!" Holmes said to the intercom. "Second target's going down. Erratic torpedo passed to port."

"Ship ahead, coming in to ram!" Bellinger shouted. It was the second ship in the starboard column. It turned its searchlight on *Swordray*.

"Right full rudder," Holmes said.

Still making flank speed, *Swordray* veered sharply to starboard, racing across the towering bow of the transport.

"We're going to make it!" Bellinger cried, eyes riveted on the ship's bow. It passed five feet off *Swordray*'s stern.

"Left full rudder," Holmes said as *Swordray* pulled clear of the starboard column into open sea. "Make ready the stern tubes. Ahead two-thirds. Open the outer doors. Stand by for third target."

"Two destroyers coming up from astern," the lookout Strong shouted.

Holmes fed a steady stream of data to the conning tower. They would shoot at only a single target this time.

"Incoming mail!" Slack cried out. The destroyers were firing. Two shells exploded off *Swordray*'s starboard bow.

"Fire seven, eight, nine and ten," Holmes calmly ordered. "Ten-second intervals."

The torpedoes swished away into dark waters, leaving four steamy parallel wakes.

"Ahead flank, right full rudder," Holmes said, watching the torpedo wakes bearing down on the target—

another transport—and trying not to think about the shell splashes.

Two of the four torpedoes hit the transport, both amidships. The ship lifted, then broke in half. The two huge sections sank instantly.

A shell fell close, then another. Holmes "chased the splashes" to confuse the Japanese gunners. But the faster destroyers were drawing ever closer.

"Clear the bridge," Holmes shouted through cupped hands. "Clear the bridge. Dive! Dive!"

With flank speed on, *Swordray* went down like a shot. "Three hundred feet," Holmes ordered from the conning tower.

As they were passing 150 feet, the destroyers caught up and dropped. WHAM. WHAM. WHAM. WHAM. Bellinger logged twelve charges in this first pass. The depth charges were set to explode too shallow and *Swordray* escaped with no damage. After she leveled off at 300 feet, Holmes took evasive maneuvers but he could not shake the destroyers. They kept *Swordray* pinned down until dawn. By then, the invasion fleet was far away—too far to catch for a second attack.

Later that day, Tom Bellinger finished logging the attack, pulling together all the data. Ten torpedoes expended, one erratic; three transports sunk. He added an unofficial postscript: "The most daring attack and skillful seamanship yet seen in the war."

4

During the next three days the radio messages from Wilkes were uniformly grim. The Japanese landed on Java against weak opposition and quickly overran the island. Wilkes and his staff retreated to Fremantle, Australia in *Holland*. *Houston* and *Perth* were sunk trying to escape to the Indian Ocean. *Perch*, fatally damaged, had been scuttled by her skipper; the crew captured. In the entire Far East, only MacArthur's garrisons in the Philippines still held out.

Wilkes ordered the surviving submarines of the Asiatic sub force to continue patrolling in the Java Sea. But, one by one, they reported materiel failures or other difficulties, aborted their patrols and limped to Australia. Ten days after the fall of Java, only two remained on combat patrol north of the Malaya Barrier: *Swordray* and *Shark*. And there seemed to be a problem with *Shark*.

Phillips laid a radio message on the wardroom table and said to Holmes, "This is the fifth message from the Commodore to *Shark* in the last five days. She still isn't answering."

Holmes scanned the message. It was an order to *Shark* to terminate her patrol and set course for Australia. Such an order required *Shark* to break radio silence and acknowledge receipt of the message. That she had failed on five successive nights to respond to the message indicated something drastic was wrong.

Phillips said, "I'm afraid *Shark* has had it."

"It looks that way," Holmes conceded grimly. Lou Shane, the skipper, was a close friend.

"Your relief," Phillips said.

"I guess the Commodore will have to find someone else," Holmes said.

"Let's hope he can't," Phillips said. "Or better yet, let's hope *he's* relieved before we get to Fremantle."

The radioman, Art Evans, brought in an urgent priority message for *Swordray*.

SHARK OVERDUE AND PRESUMED LOST. SWORD-
RAY TERMINATE ACTIVE PATROLLING. REPORT
TO CORREGIDOR TO EVACUATE MACARTHUR AND
STAFF. EN ROUTE STOP AT CEBU. OFFLOAD SPARE
TORPEDOES. PICK UP FOOD SUPPLIES AND DELIVER
TO CORREGIDOR. RELOAD TORPEDOES FROM
CANOPUS. WILKES.

Holmes passed the message to Phillips, who could not have been more excited. He said, "This time I'll bring Anne Simpson out—even if I have to kidnap her."

5

Swordray approached the harbor at Cebu warily; submerged with the crew at battle stations.

Holmes did not know whether the island had surrendered or not. At the periscope, he examined the harbor.
He saw several bombed-out rusting hulks, but no ship
afloat, nor any sign of life anywhere. He studied the deserted main pier. There was a flag on a pole, but there
was not a breath of wind and he could not tell if it were
American or Japanese.

"All stop," he said, periscope fixed on the flagpole.
Gradually *Swordray* lost what little way she had.

"Sounding," Holmes said.

"Fifteen fathoms." Ninety feet.

"Ah," Holmes said. "A faint breeze is making up.
She's beginning to flap. There it is! It's ours."

After dark, Holmes surfaced the boat and brought
her slowly into the harbor. There was still no sign of life
anywhere. Had the island been completely evacuated?
Easing into the pier, Holmes sounded repeated blasts on
the foghorn. Finally he saw a figure in the gloom at the
foot of the dock, approaching cautiously, carbine held
level. The figure stopped and shouted, "What ship?"

"Swordray," Holmes shouted back. "American submarine."

Holmes saw the man wave his arm, beckoning to men
behind him. As the group cautiously came out on the pier,
Holmes observed they were American soldiers. The man
who had challenged them was an infantry captain.

"We've come to pick up some food for Corregidor,"
Holmes said to the captain. "Do you know anything about
it?"

"No," the captain said. "Not a thing. A little Australian coastal freighter put in here last week on her way to
Corregidor. But the Captain refused to go farther. He
off-loaded about ten tons of rice into that warehouse over
there. Maybe that's what you want. Sorry about our
welcome—but you can't be too careful these days."

"I'll take whatever food you can spare," Holmes said.

"Be my guest."

"Can you give us a working party?"

"Sure, buddy."

The captain provided thirty men. While *Swordray*'s crew off-loaded her spare torpedoes, the soldiers carried the bags of rice from the warehouse to the boat. By dawn, the task was finished. For the second time in a month, *Swordray* had been converted to a supply ship. An hour before sunrise, *Swordray* backed away from the pier.

"Good luck," the infantry captain called out from the pier. "Give our best to the General."

"The same to you," Holmes replied, thinking he would certainly need luck. There was no way that small American garrison could defend Cebu against a determined Japanese assault.

6

When *Swordray* reached Corregidor under cover of darkness, Commander Earl Sackett of *Canopus* was again waiting on the pier. This time he was not so optimistic. After the arrival pleasantries, he said, "About half the men on Bataan are out of action from starvation and disease. It's only a matter of time now."

"How long?" Holmes asked.

"Two or three weeks at the most," Sackett said. "I suggest you unload and get out of here before dawn. The bombing is heavy now. And accurate."

"I assume the General's ready to leave then?"

"I assume so."

"I'd better get right over there," Holmes said.

"I'll arrange a car."

Phillips accompanied Holmes to Malinta Tunnel. Even in the dark they could see the bomb damage. The Rock was being pulverized.

Phillips went off to find Anne Simpson and Holmes made his way directly to MacArthur's bay. General Southerland escorted Holmes into MacArthur's office. They found the General on his hands and knees, playing with his small son Arthur, as cheerful as if he had not a care in the world.

"Well, Holmes!" MacArthur exclaimed affably, getting to his feet. "You're back!" Southerland escorted the boy from the room.

"We've brought more food and . . ."

"Thank God!" MacArthur said, putting his arm around Holmes's shoulder. "Our rations are rapidly depleting."

"I'm afraid it's not much, sir," Holmes said. "Ten tons of rice we picked up in Cebu."

"Are other submarines on the way?"

"I don't know, sir."

"I'm sure they must be."

"Our boats are wearing out," Holmes said. "They've been operating without respite for three months. They all need a navy yard overhaul. Four have been lost." He paused and continued, "Sir, my main reason for being here is that I have been given orders to evacuate you, your family and your staff."

"Sit down, Holmes," MacArthur said. He returned to his desk and lit his pipe. He continued, "My choice was to fight to the finish—suffer the fate of the garrison. But I have been ordered by the President to evacuate to Australia, form a new army and lead it back here to crush Homma and drive him from the Philippines. You understand that I would never have thought of deserting my men without direct orders of the Commander in Chief."

"Of course, sir," Holmes said, embarrassed by this revelation. He wondered why MacArthur felt compelled to rationalize his actions to so junior an officer.

"These are direct orders from President Roosevelt," MacArthur stressed.

"I understand, sir," Holmes said. "It's a great honor for *Swordray* to embark the General. Are you ready to go, sir?"

"I'm sorry to say I'll not be going out with you," MacArthur said. "I've decided to go out by PT boat."

"What?" Holmes blurted. "Why, sir, you can't do that. You'd never make it."

"Your PT man here, Bill Bulkeley, has assured me he

can make it." He laughed. "Not all the way to Australia, of course. Only four or five hundred miles to the south— to Mindanao. B-17s will land there and pick us up."

"Sir, I must raise the strongest objections. Those PTs are worn out—too frail for a long sea voyage."

MacArthur stared at the ceiling a moment, then said, "Holmes, can you keep a military secret?"

"Yes, sir. Of course."

"I have extreme claustrophobia," MacArthur said. "I couldn't stand to be confined in a submarine. That's top secret."

"I see, sir," Holmes replied.

"Besides that," the General went on, "I want to show your admirals that the so-called Jap blockade *can* be penetrated. Even by a lowly PT boat!"

So that was it, Holmes thought. Shove it to the Navy.

"It's not been your Navy's finest hour," MacArthur said, bitterness edging into his voice.

"I know, sir."

"What's wrong? Why can't you fight? Even the submarines let me down."

"Sir, I could be court-martialed for saying this, but our torpedoes are defective."

"What?" the General exclaimed, all ears.

"Yes, sir. They run too deep for the magnetic exploder to work."

"Can't you set them to run shallower?"

"Yes, sir. But Commodore Wilkes has refused to let us."

"Why?" MacArthur demanded.

"He has blind faith in the weapon," Holmes said. "And, well sir, he's too worn out to think clearly, or make judgments."

"I see," MacArthur said, nodding. "I'll look into that when I get to Australia."

"Sir, may I suggest again that you go with us? It would be much safer, I assure you."

"Thank you, Holmes, but my mind is made up. I'm going out by PT boat."

He rose and again put his arm around Holmes' shoulder. "I thank you from the bottom of my heart for the food. That will help sustain my men until I get back. I'm putting you—and all your crew—in for a Silver Star."

"But, sir," Holmes protested, "you already did that—last time."

"I know," MacArthur said gravely, "but you and your men have again demonstrated exceptional valor. Risking your lives to help my men. Another medal is small reward, but I have nothing else to give. Now, in place of my party, I want you to evacuate High Commissioner Sayre, his family and his small staff to Australia."

7

Phillips found Anne Simpson, as he had found her before, sitting at her typewriter amid packing crates. He leaned over her shoulder as if to read what she was typing. She turned, annoyed. Then she saw him.

"George!" she cried ecstatically, leaping up, embracing him with all her strength. Then they kissed fervently.

At length, she managed to speak. "What are you doing here?"

"We've come to evacuate the General and his family," Phillips said. "And you. You're leaving this place even if I have to shanghai you."

8

Tom Bellinger went aboard *Canopus* to draw charts of Australia. In the passageway, he ran headlong into a man who looked familiar, a skinny yeoman. The yeoman stopped, stared and then said, as though he'd seen a tarantula, "You're Thomas Bellinger!"

"Well, who the hell are you?" Bellinger asked.

"Yeoman Andrews," the man said. "I was with Lieutenant Weller when he interviewed you in the Cavite brig."

Bellinger felt a sudden chill. This was the man he had carried to the hospital in Cavite.

"What are you doing out of custody?" Andrews said, eyes narrowing.

"Fighting the goddamned war," Bellinger said, walking on.

He found the chart locker. It was manned by an old friend, Chief Slaughter.

"Tom Bellinger!" Slaughter said, extending a hand. "What the hell are you doing here?"

"We brought in some more food," Bellinger said. "And we're taking out the General and his family."

"Dugout Doug?" Slaughter said. "He's bugging out? Leaving his men?"

"That's the straight dope," Bellinger said.

"I'll be damned," Slaughter said.

"You got any charts of Australia—west coast?"

"Sure," Slaughter said. He looked up the number in the index and then began pulling charts from the thin wide drawers. Bellinger rolled the charts and secured them with a rubber band. As he was rolling up the last chart, Yeoman Andrews and two SPs entered the chart locker.

"That's the man," Andrews said, pointing to Bellinger.

"You're under arrest," the senior SP said.

"You're crazy!" Bellinger said, heart beating wildly. "What for?"

"Espionage—and escape," the SP said, opening a pair of handcuffs. Chief Slaughter watched, bug-eyed.

"That was all a mistake," Bellinger said. "A mix-up. Ask my captain—Commander Holmes."

"Not according to the yeoman here," the SP said. "Now, you want to go quietly, or . . . ?"

They handcuffed Bellinger and led him to the *Canopus* brig.

Chapter Ten

1

"Have you seen Bellinger?" Holmes asked Phillips.

Phillips replied, "He went over to *Canopus* to draw some charts about an hour ago. He should have been back by now."

"I want him to take charge of bunking down the Sayre party," Holmes said. "Maybe you'd better see if you can find him."

"Right, Captain."

Phillips made his way to the chart locker on *Canopus*. Chief Slaughter met him at the door.

"Is Bellinger here?"

"I was just on my way to *Swordray*," Slaughter said, handing Phillips the roll of charts. "He was arrested."

"What! Why?"

Chief Slaughter described what had happened.

"That's all pure bullshit," Phillips said angrily. "Where's the brig?"

Chief Slaughter led Phillips to the brig in the fo'c'sle. Two SPs on guard refused Phillips permission to see Bellinger. Phillips went immediately to find Earl Sackett.

"I'm sorry, George," Sackett said. "I don't have jurisdiction over the brig. Sixteen District headquarters took it over."

"Where are they?"

"In Malinta Tunnel."

Phillips turned to Slaughter. "Go down to the boat

and tell Commander Holmes what happened. Tell him I've gone to the tunnel."

After some difficulty, Phillips finally located 16th Naval District headquarters, then the chief of O.N.I., Captain Graves. Without ceremony, Phillips said, "You people are holding one of our men on an absurd charge."

"If you mean Quartermaster Bellinger," the captain returned loftily, "the charge is not ridiculous. It's espionage. When I was at the Naval Academy, they taught me that that was a fairly serious crime, especially in wartime. We were lucky to find him. We've been looking for him ever since he escaped from Cavite brig."

Holmes arrived ten minutes later, demanding Bellinger's immediate release. But Captain Graves was implacable. He would not even grant them permission to see Bellinger or send him a note. Holmes and Phillips had finally to concede defeat. Time had run out. If they were to leave before daylight, they must leave now.

2

A PT boat escorted *Swordray* through the mine fields to open sea. That boat will never deliver MacArthur to Mindanao, Holmes thought. It was an insane plan.

Near the end of the passage Holmes saw the PT boat blinker tube winking red. The message read:

JAP PATROL DEAD AHEAD. THREE DESTROYERS. SUGGEST YOU DIVE. WE ARE ATTACKING. GOOD LUCK.

"He's going to attack a destroyer patrol," Holmes said to Phillips via intercom.

Holmes saw the PT throw on full power, kicking up a huge phosphorescent rooster tail in its wake. Crazy fools, Holmes thought. That's suicidal.

"We better go to battle stations," Holmes said, pulling the red bridge alarm.

Through his binoculars, Holmes watched the PT's

bright rooster tail approaching the three destroyers. One of the destroyers turned a searchlight directly on the little boat.

"They've got him in the light, George," Holmes said to the intercom.

Holmes watched the PT launch its four torpedoes at high speed, then turn away sharply. All three destroyers were now firing guns at the retreating PT. One shell hit dead on and the PT blew sky high, spewing flaming gasoline all across the water.

"They got him," Holmes reported, wincing inwardly. "There can't be any survivors. Bellinger! Be sure you log this."

"Reed, sir," Les Reed reminded.

"Oh, yes. Sorry, Reed."

"I'm logging it, sir."

At that moment one of the destroyers blew apart.

"My God!" Holmes cried, less calmly than usual. "George, the PT got one of the tin cans!"

"Aye, Captain."

"What guts!" Holmes exclaimed. "You're getting all this, Reed?"

"Yes, sir."

"I'm putting that lieutenant in for a Navy Cross," Holmes said.

"Aye, sir," Reed said, scribbling madly in his notebook.

Holmes pressed the button which patched the intercom into the ship's p.a. system. "Attention ship's passengers. This is the Captain. Don't be alarmed, please. We've had a naval action up here." He described what had happened, then added, "Now we're going to dive and evade those destroyers. There is nothing for you to be concerned about. Here we go."

Holmes pulled the diving alarm. *Swordray* went deep and eased by the two surviving destroyers which were now preoccupied with rescuing survivors of their sister ship. Four hours later, *Swordray* surfaced and set course for Fremantle.

3

Phillips made his way to the chiefs' quarters, a small but private compartment in the forward battery, where the four women in the Sayre party were billeted. These were Mrs. Sayre, Anne and two other staffers.

Phillips rapped on the bulkhead. Mrs. Sayre pulled open the curtain with a smile and said, "Oh, Lieutenant Phillips." She stepped into the passageway and pulled the curtains shut.

"Is everything all right?" Phillips asked.

"I'm afraid we have three very seasick ladies in there," Mrs. Sayre said. "Your mess steward, Collins, is being very helpful. He brought a bowl of saltines. I'm afraid that's about all we can do for them."

"Yes," Phillips said. "They should be all right by tomorrow."

"It was better submerged," Mrs. Sayre said. "I had no idea you rolled so much on the surface. Will we submerge again?"

"Only for our morning trim dive," Phillips said. "Or to evade enemy planes."

"I hope my son is not driving your men crazy with all his questions. He's very mechanically inclined—and in seventh heaven."

"From what I hear," Phillips returned with a smile, "he'll be qualified in submarines by the time we reach Fremantle."

"I'm really pleased to have this opportunity to talk to you," she said. "I've heard so much about you from Anne."

"Not all bad, I hope."

"To the contrary," she said, eyes twinkling.

"Do you think I could see her for a few minutes?" Phillips asked anxiously.

"Under the circumstances, I wouldn't advise it. Not right now. Maybe when she's feeling a little better."

The radioman, Art Evans, came from the control

room with a message to *Swordray* from Commodore Wilkes. Phillips read it hurriedly and then went off to find Holmes. The message read:

> MAJOR UNITS IMPERIAL FLEET REPORTED IN TAWI TAWI ANCHORAGE. EN ROUTE YOUR DESTINATION RECONNOITER. TAKE NO OFFENSIVE ACTION. REPORT.

4

"Up scope," Holmes said.

Quartermaster Reed activated the hoist motor. Holmes grabbed the handles as they came out of the well and said, "All stop. Watch your depth." He exposed only one foot of scope above the glassy water.

It was a hot tropical day, almost cloudless. *Swordray* lay one thousand yards off Tawi Tawi, an island off the northeast coast of Borneo. Holmes took a quick sweep around the horizon, then focused on the anchorage. What he saw made him gasp inwardly.

He described it aloud. "A forest of masts. Must be most of the Imperial Fleet. There's a *Shokaku*-class carrier. And another. One, two, three, four carriers. There's a battleship tripod. One, two, three, four, five, six battlewagons . . ."

"One minute," Les Reed reminded, eye on the stopwatch.

"Down scope," Holmes said, snapping up the handles, stepping back.

Commissioner Sayre climbed up into the conning tower. He was pink-cheeked, rotund, and fresh looking in a sport shirt and white linen trousers.

"Good morning, Commissioner," Holmes said.

"Good morning," Sayre said. "Have you found anything?"

"I'd say a major portion of the Imperial Fleet is in there," Holmes returned. "Four carriers, six battleships, a dozen cruisers, two or three dozen destroyers. Would you like a quick look?"

"I certainly would."

They raised the scope and gave Sayre a look. After it had been lowered again, Sayre stroked his chin thoughtfully and said, "Is there any possibility of . . ." He paused, then went on, "If a way could be found to bottle up that fleet . . ."

"Yes," Holmes said. He had been toying with the same idea. "The water in the mouth of the cut is only sixty feet deep. If you could sink a major ship right in the mouth, it would bottle up whatever's inside."

"Exactly," Sayre said, warming to the scheme.

"A nice dream, gentlemen," Phillips cut in, "but entirely out of the question with women and a child on board. And our orders. The Commodore specifically stated, quote, take no offensive action, unquote."

"How do you assess the risk, Captain?" Sayre asked, ignoring Phillips.

Holmes thought a moment, then said, "High. If a big ship comes out, it will most likely come in daylight. It will have a destroyer screen preceding it. They'll be outside when we shoot, and probably quite close by. They'd have us dead to rights. We'd be depth-charged, probably quite severely. Perhaps fatally."

"But your Mister Phillips told me the Japs are not very persistent—and that they invariably set the charges too shallow."

"Not invariably," Holmes said. "We've lost *Perch* and *Shark*, probably to depth-charge attacks."

"If we civilians were not on board," Sayre pressed, "what would you do?"

"Frankly, sir," Holmes said, taking a deep breath, "I'd seriously consider disobeying my orders. I'd try to bottle them up."

"Excuse me a moment," Sayre said, abruptly climbing down into the control room.

Four minutes later, he was back, red-faced and puffing from the exertion. He said, "I've discussed this with Mrs. Sayre and the other ladies. They agree completely."

"Agree, sir?" Holmes asked.

"Do what you can to bottle up those ships. I'll handle the Commodore personally."

5

They lay off the Tawi Tawi cut all that day, that night and all the following day. No ships came out—or in. The weather was worsening. Strong winds and high seas assaulted them. Every indication was that a typhoon was making up.

On the second night of mounting seas, *Swordray* cruised the surface in order to charge the batteries. Suddenly the lookout's cry galvanized the bridge. "Two destroyers coming out!" The O.O.D., Fred Bohlen, instantly secured the battery charge and dived the boat. They had not been seen.

"Battle stations!" Holmes ordered when he reached the conning tower. He was still surprised that the Japanese had decided to move in darkness. And overjoyed. A night submerged attack would greatly reduce the odds of being sighted—and depth-charged.

He fixed the periscope cross hairs on the outgoing destroyers. There was a bright moon setting behind them. By the luck of the draw, *Swordray* was in perfect position to attack anything coming out of the cut.

Quite soon they could hear the destroyers thundering overhead. One, two, three, four, five, six. A full division. That meant something big was coming along behind them.

Then he saw it. It was a *Shokaku*-class carrier, perhaps even *Shokaku* itself, moving slowly from the anchorage into the cut. It loomed massively in the cross hairs, drawing ever closer. Holmes fed data to the TDC. When the range had closed to two thousand yards, he said, "Open the outer doors forward."

"Outer doors open."

"Solution on TDC," Bohlen said.

"Fire at ten-second intervals," Holmes said. "Depth set ten feet."

They fired all six torpedoes forward, then swung ship and fired all four aft tubes.

"Take her deep," Holmes commanded in his calm voice. "Rig for depth charge, rig for silent running."

As they were passing one hundred feet, number one torpedo hit the mark. The explosion was violent—and close. Its underwater force pushed *Swordray* to starboard, throwing men off their feet. Then came a second, third and fourth explosion.

"Four solid hits!" Phillips fairly shouted. "I believe we got the sonofabitch!"

Swordray passed two hundred feet and they waited for the four aft torpedoes to strike home. But there were no further explosions. Those four had missed.

"Breaking up noises, Captain," the sonarman reported.

Holmes plugged in an extra pair of padded headphones and listened intently. He heard an eerie cacophony. Boilers exploding. Hissing steam. Gear crashing on deck. There seemed no doubt about it. The carrier was plunging to the shallow bottom in the cut. He felt a wave of euphoria, but gave no outward sign of it.

"Three hundred feet," control reported. "Rigged for depth charge. Rigged for silent running."

"Very well," Holmes acknowledged, picking up the p.a. mike. He spoke into it, "All hands. This is the Captain. Sonar indicates we got four solid hits in the carrier. I believe she went down in the cut. Our yellow-bellied friends are not going to be pleased. I expect we may be in for a rough time. All hands look alive—keep on your toes. All passengers are respectfully requested to remain in their bunks."

The six destroyers turned immediately and converged pinging on *Swordray*. Each in turn made a run, dropping six depth charges. Fortunately, these thirty-six charges were set far too shallow and no harm was done *Swordray*.

After the sixth pass, Holmes ordered full speed and a due east course—away from Tawi Tawi. By then, sonar reported, the destroyers had formed a circle overhead, and the pinging skillfully overlapped. The sonarman said, "Captain, that's the first team up there."

Indeed it was, Holmes thought. The circle moved eastward with *Swordray*, precisely trailing the sub as if the waters were transparent. The destroyers made pass after pass, but the charges were still set too shallow. The hunters and the hunted were both stymied.

"Captain," Phillips said, wiping the sweat from his face with a towel. "Sooner or later, they're going to figure they're setting those charges too shallow."

"Just what I was thinking," Holmes said. "Unless we give them some food for thought." He paused and continued, "After the next pass, send up debris and dump fuel oil overboard."

After the next pass, these orders were promptly carried out. The torpedomen shot mattresses, pillows, sheets and pillow cases from the torpedo tubes. The fuel king released one thousand gallons of oil from the saddle tanks.

"They're stopping to investigate," the sonarman reported. "All converging on the debris."

"All ahead emergency," Holmes said. They had begun operations with only a partial battery charge. Until they broke free, it was vital to conserve the battery. Emergency speed would drain the battery at a great rate, but Holmes believed a five-minute burst of speed while the destroyers were diverted by the debris was worth the risk. Five minutes at top submerged speed of eight knots would put *Swordray* a little over half a mile from the destroyers.

He watched the clock. After five minutes, he said, "Ahead one-third. Sonar, report."

"Four destroyers getting underway, sir. Two still dead in the water."

"Very well."

"The four are headed this way, sir," sonar reported.

"Damn!" Phillips snarled.

"All stop. Four hundred feet."

Swordray ghosted downward another one hundred feet. The four destroyers continued on course, line abreast, all pinging. With all her air conditioning and air blowers shut down, *Swordray* was now like an oven. The intense heat was beginning to sap their strength and cloud their judgment.

"Short-scale pinging, sir," sonar reported. They could hear it through the hull. One of the destroyers had found them.

The four destroyers, deployed in a box-like formation, reconverged on *Swordray*. Then, one by one, they made a pass. WHAM! WHAM! WHAM! WHAM!

WHAM! WHAM! The explosions were deeper—and violent. Cork flew from the bulkheads. Glass dials shattered.

Holmes said quietly, "All compartments report damage."

"Sonofabitch," Phillips swore. "Those guys *are* setting them deeper."

"Would you please go below and reassure our passengers, George?" Holmes said.

Phillips quickly dropped below, thankful for an excuse to see Anne. He parted the curtain and entered the chiefs' quarters. The four women—and the young boy—were lying ashen-faced in the tiered bunks.

"Everybody okay?" he asked cheerily. He walked to Anne's bunk and took her hand. It was cold and moist. Her eyes were clouded with fear.

Six more depth charges fell close. The force of the explosion knocked Phillips to the deck and violently rolled the boat. The noise was mind-numbing.

He got to his feet and said, "Don't worry, we'll shake 'em."

Anne said in a low, quavering voice, "Are you all right, George?"

"I'm all right," he replied. "Broken leg, but I set it myself. No problem."

She smiled feebly, squeezed his hand and said, "George, I'm terrified."

"Yes, well . . . That's a perfectly normal reaction."

Six more charges fell very close. "I'd better get back," Phillips said.

In the conning tower, the sonarman said, "Captain, it's raining like hell up there. I'd say a full-blown squall."

Holmes let out a sigh of relief. The squall would toss the destroyers around and the rain falling on the water would distort the sonar.

"Ahead emergency," Holmes said.

The lights dimmed as the electrician in the maneuvering room turned the electric motors to top speed. The battery was critically low. But Holmes intended to take maximum advantage of the squall.

"Captain," control reported, "we're pulling the battery all the way down."

"Very well," Holmes said. "Give me continuous battery charge levels." He would save enough battery for emergency surfacing. No more.

"Aye, sir," control replied, adding the present reading. It was indeed critically low.

After three minutes, Holmes said, "Ahead one-third." The lights brightened.

"They've lost us, sir," the sonarman said. "Shifted to long-scale pinging. It's raining cats and dogs. A gale, I think."

"Very well," Holmes said, watching the light bulb over his head. It was slowly dimming. "All stop."

They heard six distant depth charges. Phillips smiled at Holmes. The destroyers had lost them and were depth-charging speculatively—and fruitlessly.

Watching the dimming light bulb, Holmes said, "Let's surface and use the rain as a smoke screen. I don't think they'll see us."

"Right you are, Captain," Phillips said.

"Surface!" Holmes ordered.

Swordray drained the last of her battery going up. They surfaced in a driving gale and mountainous seas. They put all four diesels on the line, two for propulsion, two for charing batteries and pulled away from Tawi Tawi at twelve knots.

Chapter Eleven

1

An Australian destroyer rendezvoused with *Swordray* thirty miles northwest of Fremantle and escorted the boat into port. They moored at a pier in the Swan River, outboard of *Seawolf* and *Sailfish*. Three high-ranking U.S. Naval officers crossed the brows and decks of the other boats and approached *Swordray*. Holmes and Phillips went down on deck to greet them.

The three were James Fife, Sunshine Murray and a third man, wearing the two-star insignia of a rear admiral. With a start, Phillips recognized the Admiral: Charles A. Lockwood, Jr. Phillips had served under Lockwood when he had commanded a peacetime submarine squadron. Phillips considered Lockwood the best submarine strategist in the U.S. Navy. On top of that, he was a genius at handling men.

"Hello, Hunt," Lockwood said genially, extending a hand to an equally startled Holmes. "How was your trip?"

Holmes shook hands with Lockwood and the others, then said, "Fine, sir. But what are you doing here? I thought you were in London."

"I've relieved John Wilkes," Lockwood said.

Thank God, Phillips said to himself, as he shook hands with the three senior officers. Thank God.

"Well, hello, Phillips," Lockwood said. "You'll be pleased to know that every gal in Australia is waiting to meet you."

Phillips blushed. At that moment, High Commissioner Sayre and the rest of his party began coming up the forward torpedo room hatch. When the introductions had been completed, Sayre said to Lockwood, "Admiral, we are deeply in your debt—in debt to the whole U.S. Navy. And I'd like to say that this submarine crew is the finest group of men I have ever met. They have performed splendidly; made our trip an absolute delight."

Anne smiled at Phillips. She was radiant.

"I'd like to second that, Admiral," Mrs. Sayre put in. "Marvelous, wonderful people."

Phillips watched the Admiral closely for his reaction. But his face was frozen in a genial noncommittal smile. After more chit-chat, Lockwood invited the entire Sayre party and Holmes and Phillips to lunch at his official quarters, Bend of the Road, where the Sayre party was to be temporarily housed. During the cocktail preliminaries, when Phillips found himself temporarily aside with Lockwood, he said, "Admiral, sir. May I see you privately after lunch?"

Lockwood registered surprise. Then he said, "Of course, Phillips. Three o'clock? That'll give us half an hour before the patrol conference."

"Yes, sir. Fine. Thank you, sir."

2

When an aide escorted Phillips into Lockwood's office, the Admiral was sitting behind his desk sifting through radio dispatches. Phillips saluted and, at the Admiral's invitation, sat down.

"Sir, I'll get right to the point," Phillips said. "Commodore Wilkes orally relieved Commander Holmes in Surabaya for insubordination. He was to take *Shark* through a yard overhaul, then . . ."

"I know," Lockwood said, nodding gravely. "The Commodore filled me in before he left."

"Well, sir," Phillips said, "the Commodore's decision was unfair. There is no finer sub skipper than Hunter Holmes. Sure, he disobeyed orders about the torpedoes, but he knows more about torpedoes than anybody else out here. After we started setting our torpedoes to run shallow, look what he accomplished in three patrols: sunk an aircraft carrier, two destroyers and four troopships. Besides that, sir, he twice carried food into Corregidor, twice evacuated key personnel and brought out the Philippine Government's gold reserves. Sir, no other skipper has accomplished anywhere near that."

Lockwood said nothing. Phillips held the floor for another ten minutes, heaping praise on his skipper. When he finally ran out of steam, Lockwood said sternly, "He disobeyed orders again at Tawi Tawi. Your instructions were specific: take no offensive action. You risked the lives of your very important civilian passengers. You can't run a navy with everybody making up his own rules as he goes along."

"Sir, Commander Holmes assessed the risk against possible gain and acted accordingly. The high commissioner—and his wife—concurred in the assessment and encouraged the Captain to make the attack."

Lockwood appeared not to be listening. Phillips felt dismay, and rising anger and frustration.

"I have a dispatch from BuOrd right here," Lockwood went on, lifting a TOP SECRET radiogram. "It states there is absolutely nothing wrong with the torpedoes."

"Screw BuOrd!" Phillips said, losing control.

"Here is something else that may interest you," Lockwood said, passing Phillips another classified paper.

Phillips read the document with total incredulity. It was a recommendation, signed by Lockwood himself, that Commander Hunter B. Holmes, U.S.N., be awarded the Medal of Honor.

"Admiral!" Phillips exclaimed. "Is this for real, sir?"

"It's for real."

"Then . . . then . . . why did you let me ramble on like that?"

"I wanted to hear what you had to say," Lockwood returned, now smiling broadly. "And I couldn't agree with you more about your skipper. That piece of work at Tawi Tawi was magnificent. You not only sank the carrier *Kyushu*, you bottled up most of the Japanese Imperial

Navy for two weeks. They had to dynamite the hulk to get
it out of the way. And they had to cancel an air strike on
Australia because of *Swordray*'s action."

"Sir, how do you know?" Phillips instantly regretted
the question. He knew the information came from the
codebreaking group they had evacuated from Corregidor.

"Coast watchers," Lockwood said, utilizing the cover
story for the codebreakers. "There is something else I want
you to know—and be thinking about. Day after tomorrow
we're going to rig a fishnet in Albany Bay and test-fire
some torpedoes, see if they run deep. I want *Swordray* to
have the honor of firing the torpedoes."

The aide entered the office and said, "Commander
Holmes is here for the patrol conference."

"Show him in," Lockwood said.

Holmes was surprised to find his exec in the admiral's
office but he had no time to think about it. Lockwood
leaped up, put out his hand and said, "Hunt, I wish to God
I had a dozen submarine skippers like you. Come on, sit
down, tell me what went wrong out there—and how we
should fight the submarine war."

3

The staff car Lockwood had provided *Swordray* pulled up
at Bend of the Road. Phillips got out and entered the
mansion. Anne was waiting for him in the massive living
room. She rose, kissed him, then said, "Did you hear the
news?"

"What news?"

"General MacArthur got out."

"Really?"

"Yes. By PT boat."

"I'll be damned. That's fantastic. I never thought he'd
do it."

"He's here in Australia. Melbourne. He said, 'I shall
return.' "

"*I* shall return? Not *we*?"

"*I* shall return."

"Megalomaniac."

"Now, George," she scolded. "You promised. I think it's really beautiful. It will mean a great deal to the Filipinos."

He changed the subject. "I've heard about a great Italian restaurant in Perth. Shall we?"

"Yes, let's."

They drove from Fremantel to Perth, making small talk. After several inquiries, they found the restaurant. It was charming; the food excellent.

"Corregidor won't last long now that the General's gone," Phillips said. "They'll throw in the towel."

"I'm afraid you're right."

"Poor Tom Bellinger," Phillips sighed. "Railroaded straight into a POW camp for the duration—if not worse."

"If anyone survives," she said, "it'll be Tom."

"I certainly hope so," Phillips said, sipping his wine. "And I'll never rest until we clear up that stupid mess."

After the waiter brought the antipasto, Phillips said, "Anne, the Admiral gave me permission to get married."

She looked fixedly at her wine glass and said, "No. Not now. Not here."

"But you said . . ."

"George," she said, turning her eyes to him. "We're leaving tomorrow for Washington."

"*What?*"

"Yes. I'm sorry. The President sent his plane for the Sayre party."

"But you can go later."

"No, I can't. He's got to write a long report on what happened. Appear before a dozen congressional committees. He needs me."

"I need you."

"To play."

"To love."

"I have a job," she said. "A duty. You have a job. The jobs come first."

"But . . ."

"After the war," she said, taking his hand in hers.

4

On Lockwood's instructions, James Fife supervised the rigging of the fishnet in Albany Bay. Lockwood, Sunshine Murray and other submarine staff officers embarked on *Swordray*.

"Open the outer door on tube one," Holmes commanded from the periscope. "Mark range!"

The cross hairs were fixed on a red flag flying from one of the large metal buoys supporting the fishnet.

"One-four-oh-oh." That was the predetermined range for the test firing. "Depth set twenty feet," Holmes said. Then, "Fire one."

The torpedo wooshed out. Holmes followed its steamy wake at the periscope. "Hot, straight and normal, Admiral," he said to Lockwood who was standing beside him.

Forty seconds later, Holmes reported, "The tug is signaling a hit in the net, admiral." James Fife was riding the tug.

"All right," Lockwood said. "Let's see what we've got."

They surfaced near the tug, whose crew was now engaged in pulling up the net. After a time, Fife megaphoned to Lockwood and Holmes on *Swordray*'s bridge, "Penetrated the net at thirty-five feet."

Holmes broke into a broad grin. As everybody but Wilkes knew, the torpedoes were running fifteen feet too deep. But Lockwood was not yet ready to celebrate the discovery. "One shot does not a test make," he remarked cautiously.

On Lockwood's orders, Holmes fired a total of ten torpedoes at a succession of nets. On average, the torpedoes ran as the first: fifteen feet below set depth. On the return trip to Fremantle, Lockwood drafted a scathing dispatch to BuOrd, reporting the results of the test and demanding that BuOrd take immediate corrective action.

As they sat in the wardroom, Holmes said quietly, "Admiral, had this test been made in Manila Bay, when the magnetic exploder was issued, the whole course of the war might have changed."

"Yes, I know," Lockwood said with an impatient sigh.

"And a lot of good skippers would not have been sacked," Holmes said.

Ten, so far, had been relieved for "lack of aggressiveness." Holmes did not doubt that most had failed because they had lost faith in their torpedoes but refused to disobey orders and set them to run shallow.

"It's a scandal," Lockwood said, "an absolute damned scandal. Somebody ought to be hanged."

Phillips wanted to shout, "Commodore Wilkes!" but he curbed that impulse.

5

On March 29, 1942, Seaman Ed Strong had the topside deck watch. *Swordray* had been undergoing refit in Fremantle for three weeks and she was nearly ready for her fourth war patrol. At 1120—as Strong later logged it— Quartermaster Tom Bellinger crossed the brow from the pier, saluted the ensign and said to Strong, "Bellinger, Thomas, 579-26-0688, reporting for duty."

Strong stared at Bellinger bug-eyed, mouth agape. The man reporting in was skeletal thin, sunburned almost black, wearing dirty, tattered whites. But it *was* Bellinger, not an apparition.

"For Christ's sweet sake," Strong finally managed to say. "Where the fuck did you come from?"

"Corregidor," Bellinger said simply.

Without further explanation, Bellinger went below to the wardroom where Holmes and Phillips were completing some last-minute paperwork. When they saw Bellinger, both officers were stupefied.

"Sit down, man!" Holmes exclaimed when he found his voice. "Collins! Bring Bellinger a cup of coffee."

Bellinger sat down and told his story. "Things were getting pretty bad back there, Captain. The crew of *Canopus* was mobilized into infantry companies and put ashore on Corregidor with rifles and machine guns. They emptied the brig, assigning everybody to the infantry. Even me. Well, sir, I got to thinking. I said to myself, Tom Bellinger, those slant-eyed bastards are not going to take any prisoners. You're going to die on the Rock, accused of espionage. My name ruined—for all time.

"About three days after we were put ashore, I found an old liberty launch abandoned in the bush. It was riddled by machine-gun fire, but the engine was okay. I said to myself, if the holes could be caulked, that's my ticket out of here. In two days, I had her shipshape. I scrounged ten five-gallon cans of gas, the same amount of water, a sail and mast, a knapsack of cooked rice, a compass, some charts and a Jap flag. I invited any number of men to leave with me, but none would. They thought I was crazy—or that they would be accused of desertion in the face of the enemy.

"I motored and sailed south to Mindoro. Nobody once challenged me. I guess the Jap flag on the mast satisfied them. I pulled into little villages—not the main ports. The natives were helpful all the way, giving me gas they had salvaged from abandoned American dumps or stolen from the Japs. And food and water. From Mindoro I went to Mindanao, to the Celebes, to Timor, and finally to Darwin. I hitched a ride on a navy plane from Darwin to Fremantle. And that's about it."

Holmes and Phillips were still thunderstruck. Phillips said, "Three thousand miles by small boat in open ocean! It's fantastic."

"Behind enemy lines," Holmes added in wonderment.

"I was lucky, I guess," Bellinger said. "Perfect weather all the way."

"Amazing," Holmes said. "Absolutely amazing."

All three men fell silent for a moment. Finally, Bellinger said to Holmes, "Sir, Rosaria Martinez left Surabaya for Australia. She was not in Darwin, I know. There's hardly anybody left in Darwin. Most likely she's here in Fremantle or in Perth. I'd like permission to go ashore and try to find her. If I could get a sworn statement from her, I could give her the money and clear up those stupid charges."

"By all means," Holmes said, quickly adding, "why

don't you get the crew to help you look, Tom? Take all the men you need."

When Bellinger had left, Holmes said to Phillips, "Now there's a man I want to go to sea with. Put him in for spot promotion to chief petty officer. And if Jack Lyons finally does decide he wants a transfer to the States, let's make Bellinger chief of the boat."

"No sooner said than done, Captain," Phillips returned. "I couldn't agree with you more."

6

That afternoon, forty crewmen from *Swordray* fanned out through Fremantle and Perth, searching for Rosaria Martinez. They called at hotels, boarding houses, brothels, bars, hospitals and police stations. No one turned up the slightest trace of Rosaria. Then *Swordray* received orders to depart the next morning and the search was, of necessity, terminated, leaving Tom Bellinger in a dismal frame of mind.

On the following morning at 0600, when *Swordray*'s mooring lines were singled up preparatory to getting underway, Lockwood's staff car tore out on the dock and screeched to a halt. Out jumped Sunshine Murray, waving his arms and grinning. "Hold it," he shouted, loping toward the boat.

Holmes suspended the departure procedure, staring quizzically down at Murray.

Murray reached the side of the boat and said, "I've got a lady in the car who told the Admiral you've got something that belongs to her."

Bellinger—wearing a new CPO cap—stared down from the bridge in astonishment as Murray opened the back door of the car and helped Rosaria out.

"Rosaria!" Bellinger cried out.

"Hiya, Tom," she waved. "What's new?" She cackled loudly.

When the crewmen on deck realized it was the woman they had been desperately hunting for, they broke into a loud cheer, waving their white hats. Bellinger went

down on deck, jumped across to the pier, tightly embraced
Rosaria and then exclaimed, "Boy, am I glad to see you.
Where have you been? I've been looking all over hell and
gone for you."

"It's a long story," she said, again cackling. "But
never mind. I told you not to worry, that I'd find you."

The departure was postponed an hour. Rosaria dictated a full statement which the yeoman typed up in
quadruplicate. After she had signed the copies, Holmes
gave one copy each to Sunshine Murray, Tom Bellinger
and Rosaria, keeping the last for the ship's file. When that
was done, Holmes got Rosaria's chest from his safe and
turned it over to her.

On deck, as Rosaria was leaving, Bellinger said,
"What will you do now?"

"Open a place here in Fremantle," she said. "Where
you submariners go, I go." She cackled.

"I shall return," Tom quoted, shaking hands warmly.

Rosaria stepped across to the pier. She hesitated a
moment, then said, "There is something you should know,
Tom. I ran into Juanita. She escaped from Rabaul, but her
husband didn't. He was killed."

Bellinger stared. "Juanita? Here?"

"Yes. Here in Fremantle."

"Now I know I shall return," Bellinger said with a
grin.

She cackled hugely and walked to the car.

Swordray stood down the Swan River and entered the
Indian Ocean, setting course for the South China Sea. The
radioman, Art Evans, came on the bridge with a message.

He reported, "Captain, Bataan and Corregidor have
surrendered. We intercepted this final message from navy
radio, Corregidor."

Holmes read:

ONE HUNDRED AND SEVENTY-THREE OFFICERS
AND TWENTY-THREE HUNDRED AND SEVENTEEN
MEN OF THE NAVY REAFFIRM THEIR LOYALTY
AND DEVOTION TO COUNTRY, FAMILIES AND
FRIENDS.

Holmes could not hold back the film in his eyes. "Thank you, Evans," he said, returning the message.

Then he turned in the direction of distant Corregidor and raised his hand in salute. Lockwood's final words to him echoed in his mind: "Go out there, Hunt, give 'em hell. We fell on our face, thanks to BuOrd, but now we'll show the bastards what we're made of."

RELAX!
SIT DOWN
and Catch Up On Your Reading!

☐	13098	**THE MATARESE CIRCLE** by Robert Ludlum	$3.50
☐	12206	**THE HOLCROFT COVENANT** by Robert Ludlum	$2.75
☐	13688	**TRINITY** by Leon Uris	$3.50
☐	13899	**THE MEDITERRANEAN CAPER** by Clive Cussler	$2.75
☐	12152	**DAYS OF WINTER** by Cynthia Freeman	$2.50
☐	13176	**WHEELS** by Arthur Hailey	$2.75
☐	13028	**OVERLOAD** by Arthur Hailey	$2.95
☐	13220	**A MURDER OF QUALITY** by John Le Carre	$2.25
☐	11745	**THE HONOURABLE SCHOOLBOY** by John Le Carre	$2.75
☐	13471	**THE ROSARY MURDERS** by William Kienzle	$2.50
☐	13848	**THE EAGLE HAS LANDED** Jack Higgins	$2.75
☐	10700	**STORM WARNING** Jack Higgins	$2.25
☐	13880	**RAISE THE TITANIC!** by Clive Cussler	$2.75
☐	12855	**YARGO** by Jacqueline Susann	$2.50
☐	13186	**THE LOVE MACHINE** by Jacqueline Susann	$2.50
☐	12941	**DRAGONARD** by Rupert Gilchrist	$2.25
☐	13284	**ICEBERG** by Clive Cussler	$2.50
☐	12810	**VIXEN 03** by Clive Cussler	$2.75
☐	14033	**ICE!** by Arnold Federbush	$2.50
☐	11820	**FIREFOX** by Craig Thomas	$2.50
☐	12691	**WOLFSBANE** by Craig Thomas	$2.50
☐	13017	**THE CHINA SYNDROME** by Burton Wohl	$1.95
☐	12989	**THE ODESSA FILE** by Frederick Forsyth	$2.50

Buy them at your local bookstore or use this handy coupon for ordering:

Bantam Books, Inc., Dept. FBB, 414 East Golf Road, Des Plaines, Ill. 60016

Please send me the books I have checked above. I am enclosing $_____ (please add $1.00 to cover postage and handling). Send check or money order —no cash or C.O.D.'s please.

Mr/Mrs/Miss_____

Address_____

City_____ State/Zip_____

FBB—6/80

Please allow four to six weeks for delivery. This offer expires 12/80.

Join the Allies on the Road to Victory
BANTAM WAR BOOKS

These action-packed books recount the most important events of World War II. Specially commissioned maps, diagrams and illustrations allow you to follow these true stories of brave men and gallantry in action.

Join the Allies on the Road to Victory
BANTAM WAR BOOKS

These action-packed books recount the most important events of World War II. Specially commissioned maps, diagrams and illustrations allow you to follow these true stories of brave men and gallantry in action.

Bantam Book Catalog

Here's your up-to-the-minute listing of over 1,400 titles by your favorite authors.

This illustrated, large format catalog gives a description of each title. For your convenience, it is divided into categories in fiction and non-fiction—gothics, science fiction, westerns, mysteries, cookbooks, mysticism and occult, biographies, history, family living, health, psychology, art.

So don't delay—take advantage of this special opportunity to increase your reading pleasure.

Just send us your name and address and 50¢ (to help defray postage and handling costs).

BANTAM BOOKS, INC.
Dept. FC, 414 East Golf Road, Des Plaines, Ill. 60016

Mr./Mrs./Miss_____
(please print)

Address_____

City_____State_____Zip_____

Do you know someone who enjoys books? Just give us their names and addresses and we'll send them a catalog too!

_____

Mr./Mrs./Miss_____

Address_____

City_____State_____Zip_____

_____

Mr./Mrs./Miss_____

Address_____

City_____State_____Zip_____

FC—9/78